ALSO BY GRAHAM SWIFT

Mothering Sunday

Mothering Sunday

A Romance

Graham Swift

ALFRED A. KNOPF
New York
2016

THIS IS A BORZOI BOOK
PUBLISHED BY ALFRED A. KNOPF

Knopf, Borzoi Books, and the colophon are
registered trademarks of Penguin Random House LLC.

Library of Congress Cataloging-in-Publication Data
Names: Swift, Graham, [date] author.
Title: Mothering Sunday : a romance / Graham Swift.
Description: First edition. | New York:
Alfred A. Knopf, 2016
Identifiers: LCCN 2015033402
ISBN 978-1-101-94752-4 (hardback)
ISBN 978-1-101-94753-1 (ebook)
Subjects: | BISAC: FICTION/Literary. | FICTION/
Historical. | GSAFD: Love stories.
Classification: LCC PR6069.W47 M68 2016 |
DDC 823/.914—dc23 LC record available at
http://lccn.loc.gov/2015033402.

Jacket photograph by Tory Smith /
Millennium Images, UK
Jacket design by Megan Wilson

Manufactured in the United States of America
First United States Edition

For Candice

You *shall* go to the ball!

Mothering Sunday

ONCE UPON A TIME, before the boys were killed and when there were more horses than cars, before the male servants disappeared and they made do, at Upleigh and at Beechwood, with just a cook and a maid, the Sheringhams had owned not just four horses in their own stable, but what might be called a "real horse," a racehorse, a thoroughbred. Its name was Fandango. It was stabled near Newbury. It had never won a damn thing. But it was the family's indulgence, their hope for fame and glory on the racecourses of southern England. The deal was that Ma and Pa—otherwise known in his strange language as "the shower"—owned the head and body and he and Dick and Freddy had a leg each.

"What about the fourth leg?"

"Oh the fourth leg. That was always the question."

For most of the time it was just a name, never seen, though an expensively quartered and trained name. It had been sold in 1915—when he'd been fifteen too. "Before you showed up, Jay." But once, long ago, early one June morning, they'd all gone, for the strange, mad expedition of it, just to watch it, just to watch Fandango, their horse, being galloped over the downs. Just to stand at the rail and watch it, with other horses, thundering towards them, then flashing past. He and Ma and Pa and Dick and Freddy. And—who knows?—some other ghostly interested party who really owned the fourth leg.

He had a hand on her leg.

It was the only time she'd known his eyes go anything close to misty. And she'd had the clear sharp vision (she would have it still when she was ninety) that she might have gone with him—might still somehow miraculously go with him, just him—to stand at the rail and watch Fandango hurtle past, kicking up the mud and dew. She had never seen such a thing but she could imagine it, imagine it clearly. The sun still coming up, a red disc, over the grey downs, the air still crisp and cold, while he shared with her, perhaps, a silver-capped hip flask and, not especially stealthily, clawed her arse.

BUT SHE WATCHED him now move, naked but for a silver signet ring, across the sunlit room. She would not later in life use with any readiness, if at all, the word "stallion" for a man. But such he was. He was twenty-three and she was twenty-two. And he was even what you might call a thoroughbred, though she did not have that word then, any more than she had the word "stallion." She did not yet have a million words. Thoroughbred: since it was "breeding" and "birth" that counted with his kind. Never mind to what actual purpose.

It was March 1924. It wasn't June, but it was a day like June. And it must have been a little after noon. A window was flung open, and he walked, unclad, across the sun-filled room as carelessly as any unclad animal. It was his room, wasn't it? He could do what he liked in it. He clearly could.

And she had never been in it before, and never would be again.

And she was naked too.

March 30th 1924. Once upon a time. The shadows from the latticework in the window slipped over him like foliage. Having gathered up the cigarette case and lighter and a little silver ashtray from the dressing table, he turned, and there, beneath a nest of dark hair and fully bathed by sunshine, were his cock and balls, mere floppy and still sticky appendages. She could look at them if she liked, he didn't mind.

But then he could look at her. She was stretched out naked, except for a pair—her only pair—of very cheap earrings. She hadn't pulled up the sheet. She had even clasped her hands behind her head the better to look at him. But he could look at her. Feast your eyes. It was an expression that came to her. Expressions had started to come to her. Feast your eyes.

Outside, all Berkshire stretched out too, girded with bright greenery, loud with birdsong, blessed in March with a day in June.

He was still a follower of horses. That is, he still threw money away on them. It was his version of economising, to throw money away. For nearly eight years he'd had money for three, in theory. He called it "loot." But he would show he could do without it. And what the two of them had been doing for almost seven years cost, as he would sometimes remind her, absolutely nothing. Except secrecy and risk and cunning and a mutual aptitude for being good at it.

But they had never done anything like this. She had never been in this bed before—it was a single bed, but roomy. Or in this room, or in this house. If it cost nothing, then this was the greatest of gifts.

Though if it cost nothing, she might always remind him, then what about the times when he'd given her sixpences? Or was it even three-pences? When it was only just beginning, before it got—was it the right word?—serious. But she would never dare remind him. And not now any-way. Or dare throw at him the word "serious."

He sat on the bed beside her. He ran a hand across her belly as if brushing away invisible dust. Then he arranged on it the lighter and ash-tray, retaining the cigarette case. He took two cigarettes from the case, putting one in her own proffered, pouting lips. She had not taken her hands from the back of her head. He lit hers, then his. Then, gathering up the case and lighter to put on the bedside table, he stretched out beside her, the ashtray still positioned halfway between her navel and what these days he would happily, making no bones about it, call her "cunt."

Cock, balls, cunt. There were some simple, basic expressions.

It was March 30th. It was a Sunday. It was what used to be known as Mothering Sunday.

"WELL, you have a gorgeous day for it, Jane," Mr. Niven had said as she brought in fresh coffee and toast.

"Yes, sir," she'd said and she'd wondered quite what he meant by "it" in her case.

"A truly gorgeous day." As if it were something he had generously provided. And then to Mrs. Niven, "You know, if someone had told us it was going to be like this, we might as well have all packed hampers. A picnic—by the river."

He said it wistfully, yet eagerly, so that, putting down the toast rack, she'd thought for an instant there might actually be a change of plan and she and Milly would be required to pack a hamper. Wherever the hamper *was*, and whatever they were supposed to put in it at such inconsiderate notice. This being *their* day.

And then Mrs. Niven had said, "It's March, Godfrey," with a distrusting glance towards the window.

Well, she'd been wrong. The day had only got better.

And anyway the Nivens had their plan, on which the weather could only smile. They were to drive to Henley to meet the Hobdays and the Sheringhams. Given their common predicament—which only occurred once a year and only for a portion of one day—they were all to meet for lunch at Henley and so deal with the temporary bother of having no servants.

It was the Hobdays' idea—or invitation. Paul Sheringham was to marry Emma Hobday in just two weeks' time. So the Hobdays had suggested to the Sheringhams an outing for lunch: an opportunity to toast and talk over the forthcoming event, as well as a solution to Sunday's practical difficulty. And then because the Nivens were close friends and neighbours of the Sheringhams and would be honoured guests at the wedding (and would have the same difficulty), the Nivens—as Mr. Niven had put it to her when first notifying her of these arrangements—had been "roped in."

This had all made clear one thing she knew already. Whatever else Paul Sheringham was marrying, he was marrying money. Perhaps he had to, the way he got through his own. The Hobdays would be paying in two weeks' time for a grand wedding, and did you really need to celebrate a forthcoming celebration? Not unless you had plenty to spare. It might demand nothing less than champagne. When Mr. Niven had mentioned the hamper he had perhaps been wondering how much the Hobdays' liberality could be relied on or how much the day might involve his own pocket.

But that the Hobdays had plenty to spare pleased her. It had nothing to do with her, but it pleased her. That Emma Hobday might be made of five-pound notes, that the marriage might be an elaborate way of obtaining "loot," pleased or, rather, consoled her. It was all the other things it might entail that—even as Mr. Niven explained about the "roping in"—gnawed at her.

And would Mister Paul and Miss Hobday be joining the party themselves? She couldn't really ask it directly, vital as it was to her to know. And Mr. Niven didn't volunteer the information.

"Would you mention these arrangements to Milly? None of it of course need affect—your own arrangements."

It was not often that he had the occasion to say such a thing.

"Of course, sir."

"A jamboree in Henley, Jane. A meeting of the tribes. Let's hope we have the weather for it."

She wasn't quite sure what "jamboree" meant, though she felt she had read the word somewhere. But "jam" suggested something jolly.

"I hope so too, sir."

AND NOW they clearly had the weather for it, and Mr. Niven, whatever his earlier misgivings, was indeed getting rather jolly. He was going to be driving himself. He had already announced that they might as well set off soon, so they could "pootle around" and take advantage of such a lovely morning. He wouldn't, apparently, be calling on Alf at the garage, who—for the right sum—could become a convincing chauffeur. In any case, as she'd observed over recent years, Mr. Niven liked driving. He even preferred the pleasure of driving to the dignity of being driven. It gave him a boyish zest. And as he was always saying, with a whole variety of intonations, ranging from bluster to lament, times were changing.

Once upon a time, after all, the Nivens would have met the Sheringhams at Sunday service.

"Tribes" had suggested something hot and outdoors. She knew it was to be the George Hotel in Henley. It was not to be a picnic. And it might well have been a day, since it was still March, of evil gales, even snow. But it was a morning like a morning in summer. And Mrs. Niven left the table to go up to get herself ready.

She couldn't ask, even now with Mr. Niven conveniently alone, "Would Miss Hobday and . . . ?"

Even if it sounded like just a maid's idle curiosity. Wasn't the coming wedding the only current talking-point? And she certainly couldn't ask, "If not, then what other separate arrangements might the two of them have in mind?"

She didn't think that if she were one half of a betrothed couple—or at least Paul Sheringham's half—she would want, two weeks before their wedding, to attend a jamboree in Henley to be fussed over by the older generation (by what he might have called—she could see him speaking with a cigarette in his mouth and wincingly screwing up his eyes—"three bloody showers together").

But in any case, if she got no further information, it still left the problem that was peculiarly hers on this day, as Mr. Niven knew, of what to do with it. Today it was painfully peculiar. The gorgeous weather didn't necessarily help at all. It only seemed—with two weeks to go—to deepen a shadow.

She was going to say to Mr. Niven, when the moment came, that if he—if he and Mrs. Niven—didn't mind, she might not "go" anywhere. She might just stay here at Beechwood and read a book if that was all right—"her book" as she might put it, though it belonged to Mr. Niven. She might just sit somewhere in the sunshine in the garden.

She knew that Mr. Niven could only approve of such a harmless suggestion. He might even think it was a rather appealing image. And of course it would mean she'd be ready to resume her duties at once, whenever they returned. She could find something to eat in the kitchen. Milly, before she left, might even make her a sandwich. She could have her own "picnic."

And it might even have happened just like that. The bench in the nook by the sundial. Bumblebees tricked by the weather. The magnolia tree already loaded with blossom. Her book on her lap. She knew which book it would be.

So—she would put the idea to Mr. Niven.

But then the telephone had rung and—it being one of her numberless duties—she'd hastened to answer it. And her heart had soared. That was a phrase you read in books, but it was sometimes actually true of what happened to people. It was true then of herself. Her heart had soared, like some stranded heroine's in a story. Like the larks she would hear in a little while, trilling and soaring high in the blue sky, as she pedalled her way to Upleigh.

But she'd been careful to say, quite loudly, into the receiver and with her best answering-the-telephone voice that was both maid-like and somewhat queenly, "Yes, madam."

CHURCH BELLS THROBBED beneath the birdsong. Warm air wafted through the open window. He had not drawn the curtains, not even out of token delicacy to her. Delicacy to her? But it wasn't necessary. The room looked out over trees and grass and gravel. The sunshine only applauded their nakedness, dismissing all secrecy from what they were doing, though it was utterly secret.

And they had never been, in all their years of—what to call it? Intimacy? Freedom with each other?—as naked as this.

Feast your eyes, she'd dared to think, like some smuggled-in beauty. Was she a beauty? She had the red knuckles and worn-down nails of her kind. Her hair must have been all over the place. It was stuck to her forehead. Yet she'd even felt something of his imperious immodesty—as if *he* were the servant bringing her a cigarette.

And barely two hours ago she had called *him* "madam"! Since it was his voice down the telephone and, for all her sudden servant-girl giddiness, she had needed to keep her presence of mind. The door to the breakfast room was open. Mr. Niven was still occupied with toast and marmalade. Down the telephone had come quick, terse, undisobeyable instructions, while she'd said, "Yes, madam . . . No, madam . . . That's quite all right, madam."

Her heart had soared. Feast your eyes. A story was beginning.

And less than an hour later, after she'd stepped off her bicycle and he'd opened the front door for her—the front door no less, as if she were a real visitor and he were a head footman—they'd laughed at her calling him "madam." They'd laughed as she'd said it again as he ushered her in. "Thank you, madam." And he'd said, "You're

clever, Jay. Do you know that? You're clever."
That was the way he paid compliments, as if
revealing to her something she might never
have imagined.

But, yes, she was clever. Clever enough to
know she was cleverer than him. She had always,
especially in the early days, out-clevered him.
It was what he wanted, she knew it, to be out-
clevered, even in some strange way commanded.
Though it could never be said of course, or even
suggested. She would never quite erase, even
when she was ninety, her inner curtsey. There
was always the given of his princely authority.
He ruled the roost, didn't he? He'd ruled it now
for nearly eight years. He had the run. He had
the run of her. Oh yes, he was princely. She'd
helped him form the habit.

But he'd called her "clever," as they stood
together in the vestibule, almost with confessing
humility, as if he were the evident fool, the hopeless case. Outside, bordering the gravel, were
ribbons of brilliant daffodils, and inside, across
the hall, rising from a large bowl, were twists of
almost luminous white flowers. Then the door

had shut behind her, and she was alone with him inside Upleigh House at eleven on a Sunday morning. Something she'd never been before.

"WHO WAS IT, Jane?" Mr. Niven had said. He might have been thinking, from the "madam," that it was Mrs. Sheringham or even Mrs. Hobday with some change of plan.

"Wrong number, sir."

"Really, and on a Sunday," he'd said, rather meaninglessly.

Then, glancing at the clock and furling his napkin, he'd given a ceremonious cough.

"Well, Jane, after you've dealt with the breakfast things, you may go. So may Milly. But before you do—"

And with these words he'd awkwardly produced the half-crown that she knew had been waiting and that merited one of her more pronounced bobbings.

"Thank you, sir. That's very kind of you."

"Well—you have a beautiful day for it," he reiterated, and she wondered again, even a little flusteredly, what he could mean by "it."

But he looked at her only enquiringly, not searchingly. Then he drew himself up, even becoming rather official.

It was a strange business, this Mothering Sunday ahead of them, a ritual already fading, yet the Nivens—and the Sheringhams—still clung to it, as the world itself, or the world in dreamy Berkshire, still clung to it, for the same sad, wishing-the-past-back reasons. As the Nivens and the Sheringhams perhaps clung to each other more than they'd used to, as if they'd become one common decimated family.

It was strange in her case for quite different reasons, and it all elicited from Mr. Niven, as well as the half-crown, much throat-clearing and correctness.

"Milly will take the First Bicycle and leave it at the station for her return. And you, Jane . . . ?"

There were no longer horses, but there were bicycles. The two in question were virtually identical—Milly's had a slightly larger basket—but they were scrupulously known as the "first" and "second" bicycles, and Milly, as befitted her seniority, had the first one.

She herself would have the second one. She might be at Upleigh inside fifteen minutes. Though there was still the matter of formal permission—if not for going to Upleigh.

"If I may, sir, I'll just take myself off. On the Second Bicycle."

"That's what I had been assuming, Jane."

She might have just said "my bicycle," but Mr. Niven was a stickler for the "first" and "second" thing, and she'd learnt to go along with it. She knew, from Milly, that the "boys"—Philip and James—had once had bicycles (as well as horses) which had become known as the First and Second Bicycles. The boys were gone, so were their bicycles, but for some strange reason the "first" and "second" tradition had carried over to the two servants' bicycles, even though these were, necessarily, ladies' versions, without crossbars. She and Milly perhaps didn't qualify as ladies, but they qualified, in one persistent respect, as the dim ghosts of Philip and James.

She had never known Philip and James, but Milly had once known them and indeed cooked for them. And Milly had once known "her lad," who'd gone the same way as Philip and James, even perhaps in the same dreadful part of France. And her lad had been called Billy. Milly would not often use his name— "my lad" had become as obligatory as "first" and "second" bicycles—so it was hard to gauge how much she'd actually, really known him. Yet if they'd ever got married they would have been Milly and Billy. Perhaps "her lad" was a fiction of Milly's that no one could disprove, or would wish to. The war had suited all purposes.

ONCE UPON A TIME . . . Once upon a time she'd arrived, the new maid, Jane Fairchild, at Beechwood just after a great gust of devastation. The family, like many others, had been whittled down, along with the household budget and the servants. Now, there was only a cook and a maid. Cook Milly, with her seniority, had been theoretically promoted to cook and housekeeper, but she clung to the kitchen, while she, the new and inexperienced maid, soon effectively did most of the housekeeping.

She didn't mind any of this. She loved Milly.

Cook Milly was just three years her elder, but it seemed a condition of the loss of "her lad" that she'd rapidly put on weight and girth, even developed an air of scatty wisdom, and so become like the mother she'd perhaps always wanted to be. "Her lad" even began to suggest she might have been the poor boy's mother.

And today Cook Milly, if her bicycle could bear her weight to the station, was going to see her mother.

"OF COURSE you may, Jane," Mr. Niven had said, inserting the napkin into its silver ring. Was he going to ask her where she was thinking of going?

"You have the Second Bicycle at your disposal and you have—ahem—two and six. And you have the whole county at your disposal. As long as you come back again!"

Then, as if slightly envying the broad freedom

he'd just granted, he said, "It's *your* day, Jane. You may be—ahem—at your own devices." He knew, by now, that such a phrase would not be over her head—it might even have been meant as a gentle tribute to her reading habits. Cook Milly might have thought "devices" meant kitchen spoons.

He can't surely have meant anything else by it.

IT WAS March 30th 1924. It was Mothering Sunday. Milly had her mother to go to. But the Nivens' maid had her simple liberty, and half a crown to go with it. Then the telephone had rung, rapidly altering her previous plan. No, she wouldn't be having a picnic.

And it was surely more than she could ever have hoped for, since even if Mister Paul and Miss Hobday were not to be of the Henley party it had left open the question of how they might both pass the day together anyway. A question which still remained open.

They both had cars, she knew this. Young people of their kind could have cars now. He sometimes referred to hers as the "Emma-mobile." They would certainly both be at *their* own devices, and if they played their cards right they might, if it was their inclination, have at their disposal either of two helpfully emptied houses. If you thought about it, up and down the country on this day there might be any number of temporarily vacated houses available for secret assignations. And if she knew Paul Sheringham . . .

Exactly. She knew him and she didn't know him. She knew him in some ways better than anyone—she would always be sure of that—while knowing that no one else must ever know how much she knew him. But she knew him well enough to know the ways in which he was not knowable. She didn't know what he was thinking now, as he lay naked beside her. She often thought he didn't think anything.

She didn't know how he behaved with Emma Hobday. She didn't know how much Emma Hobday—Miss Hobday—knew him. She didn't know Emma Hobday. Having only glimpsed her once or twice, how could she? She knew she was pretty, in a flowery kind of way. She was the kind of woman who might be called a flower, who dressed in flowery clothes. But she had no idea what she was like, as it were, beneath the flowers. How could she? Paul scarcely spoke of her, though he was going to marry her. And that, while it showed her how much she didn't know Paul Sheringham, was a comforting mystery.

What seemed, oddly, to be happening was that the closer Paul Sheringham and Miss Hobday got to marrying, the less time they actually spent in each other's company. She had heard of that thing where brides and grooms weren't supposed to see each other for a day (or was it just a night?) before their wedding, but this was a sort of expanded version of that practice and had been going on for some time. He ought surely to make some stronger show of being the eager husband.

So the phrase had come to her, like a phrase too from a book, that had suddenly acquired actual meaning: "arranged marriage."

It was the best she could hope for. Not that it really helped her. But if, for whatever reason, a combination of flowers and money, he was slipping towards such a thing, then this day—so she had thought even as she attended to breakfast and Mr. Niven spoke about hampers—this day that had begun with such promising sunshine might be the last chance. She didn't know whether to call it his or hers, let alone theirs.

In any case she was getting ready to lose him. Was he getting ready to lose her? She had no right to expect him to see it that way. Did she have any right to think she was losing him? She had never exactly had him. But oh yes she had.

She didn't know what it would be like to lose him, she didn't want to think about it, though lose him she must. Perhaps all she was thinking on the morning of Mothering Sunday, as she brought in more coffee at Beechwood, was that if he played his cards right with this day then she wanted him to play them with her. Some hope. Then the telephone had rung. "Wrong number." Her heart had soared.

"The shower will be leaving soon. I'll be on my tod here. Eleven o'clock. Front door."

He had spoken in a strong whisper, as if picturing her exact predicament, even down to the open breakfast-room door. It was an order, a curt order, but a transforming one. And she had listened, or appeared to listen, with polite patience, as if to some ineptly garrulous caller who had not yet realised their error.

"I'm awfully sorry, madam, but you have the wrong number."

How skilled she'd become, in seven years. At imitating their "awfully"s. And at other things too. But she still had to assimilate it: just the two of them in the empty house. It had never happened before. Front door. She had never been bidden to any front door. Though sometimes, in earlier days, it might have indicated his required form of congress.

"That's quite all right, madam."

Mr. Niven's munching on his toast and marmalade had perhaps obliterated some of her flawless performance.

"Wrong number," she'd explained. And then he'd given her half a crown.

And suppose he had known what things she'd once done for Paul Sheringham—to Paul Sheringham—yes, for only sixpence, sometimes for even less. And then, after not so long, for nothing, nothing at all, mutual interest in the transactions cancelling any need for purchase.

Though when she was eighty or ninety and

was asked, as she would be, even in public interviews, to look back on her younger years, she felt she could fairly claim (though of course never did) that one of her earliest situations in life was that of prostitute. Orphan, maid, prostitute.

HE TAPPED ASH into the ashtray decorating her belly.

AND SECRET LOVER. And secret friend. He had said that once to her, "You are my friend, Jay." He had said it so announcingly. It had made her head go light. She had never been called that, named that thing so decisively by anyone, as if he were saying he had no other friend, he had only just discovered, in fact, what a friend might be. And she was to tell no one about this newly attested revelation.

It had made her head swim. She was seventeen. She had ceased to be a prostitute. Friend. It was better perhaps than lover. Not that "lover" would have been then in her feasible vocabulary, or even in her thinking. But she would have lovers. In Oxford. She would have many of them, she would make a point of it. Though how many of them were friends?

And was Emma Hobday, even though she was his bride to-be, his friend?

In any case, as friends or perhaps even as lovers, or just as young Mister Paul and the new Beechwood maid he'd spotted one day in the post office in Titherton, they'd done all sorts of things together, in all sorts of secret locations. The two houses were scarcely a mile apart, if you went by the back routes and then, necessarily, through the garden. The greenhouse and the disused part of the stables were just two of their recourses. And they'd done those things by a strangely dependable intuition—you could hardly call it a time table—that had become the habit, the telepathy of true friends. As if everything were always by imagined chance, but they knew it was not.

So—they were really lovers?

Because there was anyway such an intensity and strange gravity to their experimentation, such a consciousness at least that they were doing something wrong (the whole world was in mourning all around them), it had needed some compensating element of levity: giggling. It had sometimes seemed in fact that to get each other giggling was the real aim of it all——a dangerous aim to have when another essential factor was that they should on no account be found out.

And the remarkable thing was that even now, with his suave and superior ways and his silver cigarette case, there was a giggle still inside him, still there, even now when they'd become accomplished, unfumbling, serious-faced addicts at what they did. It might still suddenly emerge, without warning, without explanation, out of his polished exterior, an explosive cacophonous giggle, as if a mould had shattered.

But he was naked now, there was no mould to shatter. And why should he giggle? It was their last day.

SHE HAD SPED on her bicycle from Beechwood to Upleigh. That is, since Mr. and Mrs. Niven were yet to depart, she had been careful not to be seen to be hurrying at all, or to be pointing the bicycle in the direction of Upleigh. At the gate she had turned casually right not left. But then, after turning two more corners, she had sped.

Then, nearing Upleigh, she'd done something she had never done before. She had not approached by the usual back route, by the garden path—leaving her bicycle hidden in the familiar clump of hawthorns, then continuing, alertly, on foot. She had taken the front road and boldly cycled through the Upleigh gates and up the drive between the rows of lime trees and the swirls of daffodils.

It was what he had instructed—ordered her to do. The front door. It was only as she turned through the gates that the extraordinariness, the unprecedented gift of it—yes, it was *her* day—came to her. The front door! And he must have wanted to observe her do it, since hardly had she brought her bicycle to a halt near the porch than the front door—or rather one of them, there were two tall imposing glossy-black doors—opened, as if by a miraculous power of its own.

She did not know for certain, though she would soon, that his bedroom overlooked the drive. He might have been visible for a moment, had she been looking for him, at the open window on the first floor. But he was visible suddenly anyway, stepping from behind the apparently self-opening door—to be called "madam" by her, while she would be called "clever" by him. She'd propped the bicycle quickly against the front wall. The hall, beyond the vestibule, had black-and-white chessboard tiles. There were the fronds of intense white flowers.

"My mother's precious orchids. But we're not here to look at them."

And he'd led her—or rather steered her by her backside—up the stairs.

Then it might have been her turn to be called "madam," since, once inside the bedroom, he began almost immediately to undress her as he'd never done before—or rather as he'd never before had such an opportunity to do. Could it even strictly be said that he'd *ever* "undressed" her?

"Stand there, Jay. Stay still."

It seemed that he wanted her not to move, just to stand, while his fingers gradually undid and released everything and let it fall about her. So it was not at all unlike how she might sometimes, if Mrs. Niven should wearily request it, be required to "undo" Mrs. Niven. Except, she couldn't deny it, there was a reverence with which he went about the task that she could never have applied to Mrs. Niven. It was like an unveiling. She would never forget it.

"Don't move, Jay."

Meanwhile she could look around her at this remarkable room she had never been in before. A dressing table, with a triple-panelled mirror, cluttered with small objects, mainly silver. An armchair with a striped pattern, gold on cream. Curtains similarly patterned and completely drawn back (while he undressed her!) and gently stirring. An open window. A carpet of a pale grey-blue, the colour of cigarette smoke caught in sunlight—and sunlight was pouring in. A bed.

"What is this, Jay? Your hidden treasure?"

His fingers had found something in the recesses of her clothing.

A half-crown piece.

IT WAS Mothering Sunday 1924. Mr. Niven had indeed watched her unspeedily cycle off, since he'd just brought the Humber round to the front to await Mrs. Niven. She supposed that, most of the time, Mr. Niven would "undo" Mrs. Niven, if she couldn't undo herself. What a word—"undo"! She supposed that Mrs. Niven might now and then say, "Undo me, Godfrey," in a different way from how she might say it to her maid. Or that Mr. Niven might sometimes say in a different way still, "Can I undo you, Clarrie?"

She supposed that Mr. and Mrs. Niven might still, now and then ... even though some eight years ago they had lost two "brave boys." But she did not suppose. She occasionally saw the evidence. She changed the sheets.

She did not know, even on Mothering Sunday, what it would be like to be a mother and lose two sons—in as many months apparently. Or how such a mother might feel on such a day. No boys would be coming home, would they, with little posies or simnel cakes to offer?

But Paul Sheringham would be getting married in two weeks' time and he was the one son left. And of course the Nivens would be there. He was (and oh how he knew it) both families' darling.

NOW MR. AND MRS. NIVEN would be driving, sitting side by side, through the bright spring sunshine to Henley. Milly already, before any of them, had creaked her way out of the Beechwood gates to get the 10:20 from Titherton. And this house, Upleigh, was now obligingly empty, except for themselves, since Mr. and Mrs. Sheringham—"the shower"—had also departed for Henley, and the Upleigh cook and maid—Iris and Ethel—had been driven to Titherton Station by no less a person than Paul Sheringham.

Only now did he tell her this, as he undressed her—or rather, since she was soon standing naked in his sunlit room, as she, in reciprocal fashion, began to undress, to "undo," him.

"I drove Iris and Ethel to the station."

It was something that hardly needed announcing. Did it relate to what they were doing right now? And it was something—she thought later—that had hardly needed doing. On a morning like this Iris and Ethel might have been happy to walk. Upleigh was even closer to Titherton Station than Beechwood was.

Was it his way of explaining why his telephone call had come so agonisingly late? Or of assuring her that the house really was all safely theirs? He had packed off the staff himself.

But he had said it in such an untypically earnest way. As if he wished her to know, she would think later, that on this special upside-down day he had placed himself, lordliest of the lordly as he could be, in the deferring role. He had not only offered her his house, opened its door for her obediently on her arrival, then undressed her as if he were her slave, but he had, in this other way too, been of service to servants, kind to her kind.

"For the 9:40. I took them in the Ma-and-Pa-mobile."

Which would now perhaps be already parked somewhere in Henley. His own car, still in the stable-turned-garage, was a racy thing with a top that came down, only really meant for two.

Perhaps he did it every year, drove them to

the station. A Sheringham tradition. But then he said, "I wanted to give them a proper goodbye."

A proper goodbye? They might be back by teatime. They weren't going for ever.

Was it his roundabout way of saying that this was what he was giving *her*? A proper goodbye. She could hardly give it much thought at the time, since—his own clothes removed and quickly draped with hers over the armchair—they had moved, with no more ceremony, to the bed.

But she would think about it later. All her life she would picture it: the two women, awed and silent in the back of the big black saloon while he drove them, chauffeur-style. On the station forecourt he might have opened doors and helped them out with the same gracious attentiveness with which he'd removed her clothes. They might even have thought he was going to offer them each a kiss.

All her life she would try to see it, to bring back this Mothering Sunday, even as it receded and even as its very reason for existing became a historical oddity, the custom of another age. As he set them down the distant white puffs of the 9:40 to Reading might already have been visible in that brilliant blue sky. On the platform there might have been two or three others like Iris and Ethel waiting to set off on similar journeys (though not yet Cook Milly, who would get the 10:20).

All the maids. All the mothers getting out in readiness what passed for their best china. All the maids with their mothers to go to.

AND SHE KNEW the maid at Upleigh. She was called Ethel Bligh. Poor mouse. She had had conversations with Ethel—they met on errands at Sweeting's the grocer's in Titherton—conversations that scarcely became conversations and that never got near becoming gossip. The cook at Upleigh was a stout creature rather like Milly, but Ethel was a nimble-bodied maid, a little like herself. With another sort of Ethel she might not only have gossiped—the two of them leaning on their bicycles outside Sweeting's—but even giggled, even giggled just a tiny bit like she giggled with Paul Sheringham.

But even then she wouldn't have told this

other Ethel what she got up to with Mister Paul. Or rather this other Ethel would have known, guessed already. Or rather this other Ethel would have got in first, or have been got in first, being so handily under the same roof.

So it was just as well, in fact, that Ethel was not this other Ethel, but a good little maid who, without having to struggle much to do it, did what maids were constantly required to do: turned a blind eye and a deaf ear and, above all, kept a closed mouth.

Ethel might be going to her mother's today in the same spirit of meek submission with which she'd once offered her services to Mrs. Sheringham. The two things might have become indistinguishable.

Did she and Iris gossip? Surely they did. On the train after their tongue-tied car ride, did they suddenly start to talk? So what was all that about? Was it because he was getting married and would soon be—leaving them?

Or would they have sunk into deeper silence, unaccustomed as they were to being out in the world and to being reminded that they had lives, even mothers, of their own? Would they have just gawped and blinked at sun-bathed, lamb-dotted England?

While Paul Sheringham religiously undressed her.

"Stay still, Jay."

AND, EVEN AS he undressed her and as if to answer another, unspoken question of hers, he'd said, "I'm mugging up, Jay. My law books. That's what I'm doing now. Mugging up." It might have produced a giggle, from either of them, but it didn't. It was said with such an instructive urgency, as if, were she ever to be asked—interrogated—that's what she was to say that he, that they, had been doing.

It would pass into her private unconfessable code-language, standing for so much that was beyond telling anyway. She would never be able to hear the phrase lightly, even in Oxford, where a great deal of mugging up went on.

But it had been his ruse for getting out of the Henley expedition and for securing the house for himself—and her. It was also, neatly, like a virtuous pledging of his future responsibilities. When they were married he and Emma Hobday were going to live in London (this she knew and could only bleakly accept) and he was supposed to be going to make an honest man out of himself and even an honest living—regardless of his new access to "loot"—by studying to become a lawyer.

How times, indeed, could change.

So even today, even on such a glorious morning, he would demonstrate his commitment to this plan with a spot of serious mugging up. It was unlike him, it was out of character, but hardly to be objected to. Perhaps there being only two weeks left—so they might be chucklingly surmising in Henley—had brought out this sudden rush of conscientiousness in him.

Except that he knew and she knew—did Miss Hobday know?—that he had about as much intention of becoming a lawyer as becoming a lettuce.

"We're mugging up, Jay." If anyone should ask.

Though it still left one unanswered, and not even asked, question. She didn't dare ask it, or want to ask it. It was for him to say.

Assuming that he (they) would not be—

mugging up—all day, what other separate arrangement might there be, might he have in place, with Miss Hobday?

THEY LAY side by side, uncovered, flicking ash, not talking, watching the smoke from their cigarettes rise up and merge under the ceiling. For a while such smoke-sharing was enough. She thought of the white puffs from trains. Their cigarettes, now and then merely lodged vertically in their lips, were like miniature companion chimneys.

There was only the bird-chatter outside and the strangely audible, breath-held silence of the empty house, and the faint ripple of air over their bodies, reminding them, though they eyed the ceiling, that they were entirely naked. Two fish on a white plate, she thought. Two pink salmon on a sideboard, waiting for guests, guests at a wedding even, who would never arrive . . .

She did not want to say, to ask, anything that might puncture the possibility of their staying like this for ever.

It was called "relaxation," she thought, a word that did not commonly enter a maid's vocabulary. She had many words, by now, that did not enter a maid's vocabulary. Even the word "vocabulary." She gathered them up like one of those nest-building birds outside. And was she even a maid any more, stretched here on his bed? And was he even a "master"? It was the magic, the perfect politics of nakedness.

More than relaxation: peace.

With one hand, the other holding her cigarette, she just brushed, not looking, his moist cock, feeling it stir almost instantly, like some sleeping nestling. As if she might have done such a thing all her life, an idle duchess, stroking a puppy. Only moments ago, with the same hand twisted back to grasp one of the brass rods of the bedstead—this bed she'd never been in before— she'd pressed with the other hand, palm flat but fingers digging, the small of his back, pressed hard the place where it seemed his cock joined his spine. She was commanding him—what command could be stronger and more bidding? Yet he had commanded her: the front door.

Now it seemed that what they'd just done was only a doorway itself to this supreme region of utter mutual nakedness.

Peace. It was true of all days, it was the trite truth of any day, but it was truer today than on any day: there never was a day like this, nor ever would or could be again.

HER CIGARETTE WAS burning down. She moved the little ashtray—it was surely her prerogative—onto the strip of sheet between them. It was her belly, she might have said, it wasn't a table, she didn't want him stubbing his cigarette out against it—much as she might actually have liked it. And how she would remember that ashtray coolly resting on her belly.

Then she wished she hadn't been so fastidious or presumptuous, hadn't done anything at all.

He took the cigarette from his mouth and simply held it, upright, against his own belly.

"I have to meet her at half past one. At the Swan Hotel at Bollingford."

He didn't otherwise move, but it was like

the breaking of a spell. And only anyway what she must have anticipated. Though she thought she might have passed, by magic dispensation, beyond that "must." The rest of the day? One portion of it couldn't (could it?) last for ever. One fragment of a life cannot be the all of it.

She didn't stir, but she might have, inwardly, altered. As if she might have had her clothes invisibly on again, might even be turning back into a maid.

But nor did he stir, as if in his stillness countering—belying—what he'd just said. He didn't have to keep his appointment, did he? Who said so? He didn't have to do a damn thing he didn't want to, did he? He might simply lie here and ignore it.

And "her"—not "Emma." It was like some dismissal shared between them. And "I have to."

His cigarette was almost finished.

He didn't move, nor did she, as if in fact he hadn't just spoken. Yet equally as if the slightest movement on her part, let alone a sound, a word, might have been to acknowledge that he'd said it and so commit him to its consequences.

It was not her place, after all, with her ghostly maid's clothes back on again, to speak, suggest or do more than wait. Years of training had conditioned her. They are creatures of mood and whim. They might be nice to you one moment, but then— And if they snapped or barked, you must jump. Or rather take it in your stride, carry on, not seethe. Yes sir, yes madam. And always—it was half the trick—be ready for it.

Then it came to her that the whole thing might be turned the other way round. This upside-down day. She was lying here with him in his room, like his wife, and he was brazenly consulting with her as to whether he should go and see his troublesome mistress. Some couples, some of their kind, might actually do this. And wasn't it in fact, at heart, like that? He wasn't yet married. To either of them. She and Emma Hobday were equals.

He did not speak, as if enough silence after his remark, for all its apparent call for punctuality, might cancel everything. And he was perfectly capable of such contempt for nicety. Of having it both ways. He hadn't been dishonest, had he? He just hadn't acted accordingly. It was his way: he misbehaved, but he didn't lie about it.

And he'd taken Ethel and Iris nobly to the station.

And she wasn't going to say, like some remarkably forbearing wife, "Then you'd better go, hadn't you?" Was he really asking her to?

His lengthening silence might have given her an increasing power—or compliance. But the moment was passing when he might have said, "But I think we have the whole day, Jay, don't you?" Putting his hand where the ashtray had been. Or a little lower.

It must happen. He would go to her and have his lunch with her and even perhaps, somehow or other, later today, have his entitled way with her. If that is how it was between them. He might even bring her back here to do so. To this very room. She hadn't asked him when his "shower" were expected to return. He was in charge of that contingency. They would hardly yet have sat down to lunch in Henley.

And now, with his own lunch plans suddenly hovering in the air, but with their clothes still strewn together over the armchair, their moment already was passing. He didn't have that much time.

Moment? It was too mean a word. Hour? Day? Gift? But it was slipping away, as the day had already slipped away from the peak of noon. He must have looked at the little clock, or at his silver pocket watch, on the dressing table when he got up to fetch the cigarettes.

And there was the unalterable truth that it might never have happened at all. And, yes, she should be grateful, eternally grateful. "I wanted to give them a proper goodbye." She might have been touring Berkshire on a bicycle.

And he might, by the same connivance, have brought "her" here anyway. His telephone call might have been to the Hobday residence. "She" might have had to speak into the telephone just as slyly and pretendingly. Did they communicate in such ways? Then turned up here, crunching the gravel, in her car. The Emmamobile. She might be here with him *now*.

But she couldn't imagine it. Her flowery dress over the chair, her silky underwear. She was the one actually lying here, and shouldn't she be grateful? Even if he'd be lying here beside the other one later. Two in one day. Was it possible? The Swan at half past one. But she couldn't imagine it.

At the back of her mind was the scrambling thought that if his wife-to-be was in some way "arranged" then the arrangement might include that she must be a flawless, untouched virgin, as if he were marrying a vase. And unlikely as it was—that *he* could promise himself to a vase— there must be some truth in her thought or some other reason for his lack of soon-to-be-married enthusiasm. If it were not the plain fact that he was lying here now with her.

IN ANY CASE after minutes of mere stillness, of almost defiant inertia, he suddenly moved, and with an excessive upheaval of his limbs. The whole mattress rocked like a boat. He picked up the slipping ashtray and crushed the stub of his cigarette brutally against it.

And it was then, as she lifted one knee to

counter the commotion, that she felt the trickle from between her legs: his seed leaving her, along with liquid of her own. She had other words than "seed," but she liked the word "seed." It might have happened at any moment, but its happening now, along with its seeping sadness, seemed almost like a sudden riposte. Well, it would be difficult for him now to be here, later, with her, the flowery one, if that was part of his plan.

Unless he were to tell her right now—she was still a maid, if not his—to replace the sheets.

It was crude arguing. It was what animals, who made no marriage vows and kept no servants, relied on. They marked their territory.

And she wasn't going to say, now he was on his feet and the decision all but made, "Please, don't go. Please, don't leave me." She was disqualified from the upper world in which such dramas were staged. She had her lowly contempt for such stuff anyway. As if she couldn't have used—but she wasn't his wife, it was all the other way round—a different, quieter but fiercer language. Or just the bullet of a look.

In any case, there was the trickle between her legs.

He moved across the room. He might be going only to consult the time. Once again she was able to view him in his surly nakedness. Yes, he had a different walk without his clothes on, an animal walk.

He turned at the dressing table to look at her, holding his watch now in his hand. She hadn't moved, dared to move, herself. There was only her lifted, theoretically coaxing knee, only her own unhiding nakedness to make him think again. He was taking it in, no more abashed, once again, about his looking than about his own display of himself. His cock was a little fuller but still merely hanging. And now he was familiarly winding the watch, blindly dealing with it even as he gazed.

"Not quite a quarter to. If I step on it, I should make it. We're meeting halfway. The Swan. She knows the people there. It was her idea."

As if she, the Beechwood maid, knew anything about the Swan Hotel at Bollingford or how long it took to get there by car. But the party at Henley would have known? The young things were having their own private lunch. Well, you couldn't blame them. After he'd commendably spent the morning with his law books.

But there was the little matter now of his getting dressed, of his making himself presentable, of his putting together again his outward person. He seemed in no hurry to do so. He looked at her, his eyes ran up and down her. He must have surely noticed the little patch between her legs.

She'd never known him show, even when actually hurrying, any sense of haste or unseemly agitation. Except, that is—but it seemed suddenly a very long time ago—when it had all been a boy's uncurbable rush. She'd sometimes said to him, "Slow down." She'd even said, as if she were steeped in experience herself, "Slower is better."

Well, they were steeped in experience now. He had never known anyone better, she was sure of it. Nor had she. It was in the look he gave her now. And in the stare she returned.

She found it difficult, even as she stared, not to let tears come into her eyes, even as she knew that to allow them, use them, would have been somehow to fail. She must be brave, generous, merciless in allowing him this last possible gift of herself.

Would he ever forget her, lying there like that?

And he *was* in no hurry. The sun from the window lit him. A bar or two of shadow ran across his torso. He finished winding the watch. His eventual car journey must be getting impossibly fast.

She didn't know how he had acquired his sureness. Later, in her memory, she would marvel at it and be almost frightened by his possession of it then. It was the due of his kind? He was born to it. It came with having no other particular thing to do? Except be sure. But that, surely, would flood you with unsureness. On the other hand, to be a lawyer, merely a lawyer—she even felt it for him and saw him in a lawyer's imprisoning dark suit—could only take his sureness away.

She thought momentarily and madly: Supposing she—Emma, Miss Hobday—had come to get him anyway. Supposing—this was 1924, it

was the modern age—she had taken it upon herself to come here, in her car, to collect him now.
To surprise him, drag him from his "mugging
up." On such a marvellous day. Wheels on the
gravel. Her flowery voice—with a slight touch
of horse—shouting up, as she noticed the opened
window, knowing that it was his bedroom.

"Come to get you, Paul! Where are you?"

What then? She had no doubt that he would
have handled it all, somehow, surely. Even wearing just his signet ring. Even standing at the
window. "Emsie, darling! What a surprise! Give
me a mo to put a shirt on, would you?"

And how might she, the Nivens' maid in the
Sheringhams' house, have handled it?

On the dressing table beside him were all the
other little accoutrements of his life, sentimen-
tal or purposeful, each one like his own piece
of unhidden treasure. Hairbrushes and combs.
Cufflinks and studs in boxes. Photos in silver
frames. A preponderance of silver, kept bright
by Ethel. Maids had perpetually to dust round,
not to mention actually polish, such parapher-
nalia, making sure nothing was moved from

its ordained position. Well, it was easier than a woman's dressing table.

If you were brought up with such stuff attached to you, such personal insignia, then perhaps it was easy to be sure, Not to mention the contents of his wardrobe, in the adjacent dressing room—she had briefly seen it as she was bustled in. All his hanging choices. Not to mention other possessions scattered round the house.

All that she owned or wore could be put in one plain box. If she had to leave in a hurry, and she always might, she could.

But it was these little trinkets, this boys' jewellery that seemed now to claim him, confirm him. Signet ring. Pocket watch. Cufflinks. When he was dressed and before he left he would gather up the initialled cigarette case and lighter. He would run the hairbrush across his hair, apply the tortoiseshell comb. His two brothers must have taken an assortment of such things, much of it perhaps newly and morale-boostingly purchased, when they went across to France, never to come back. Ivory-handled shaving brushes, that sort of thing. They, the brothers, were on the dressing table now, in silver frames. She'd noticed them as soon as she entered the room. That must be Dick and Freddy. Both in officers' caps. She'd never seen them before. How could she have?

She'd looked at them as he'd undone her clothes.

HE PADDED OUT of the room to the bathroom. Still only the signet ring. He wasn't there for long. He had only to wash and rinse himself, whatever men did. Remove, that is, all immediate traces of herself on him. She would think about this later.

The room seemed to close in on her during his short absence, even to claim her as part of its furniture. She did not move. She lay indeed like an inanimate object, though she was all tingling flesh. He had made no sign to her that she *should* move—that now he'd got up, it might be proper for her to do the same. Rather the opposite. It was no surprise to him, when he reappeared, that she was still tenaciously lying there. It was what, it seemed, he had even expected, wanted her to do.

He had a scent about him now that she might have appreciated, save that it cancelled out the sweeter smell of his sweat. She would think about this too later: that he put on his cologne. But he was still naked and in no apparent haste. He had brought in, from the dressing room, a fresh white shirt, a pale-grey waistcoat and a tie, but it seemed that the rest of his outfit would consist of what he'd discarded on the chair. He might have done all his dressing in the dressing room, but perhaps this was his habit anyway, to dress by the light of the window, by his dressing table and its angled mirrors. The dressing room was merely a wardrobe.

But it seemed that he did not want to be separated from her, though he was about to leave. It was in some way all for her—that she should watch him dress, watch his nakedness gradually disappear. Or that he just didn't care. The sureness, the aloofness, the unaccountable unhurriedness. She should leave too? But he said nothing and she remained, as if now actually commanded to, where she was, while his eyes travelled over her again, even as he dressed.

He must have noticed the trickle. But it was part of his fine disdain not to notice it. It was like the clothes he might leave pooled on the floor, to find their way back to him, laundered and pressed, hanging in the dressing room. These were things to be cleared up discreetly by people who cleared up such things. And she, normally, was such a one. She was part of the magic army that permitted such disregard. Was he really going to tell her, before he left, to deal with the mess? And give her her cheap moment to remind him that she was not his servant?

But she saw as he looked at her—and surely at that incriminating patch—that such a squalid little scene was far from his thoughts. Some other kind of indifference was making him careless of such a minor matter as a stain on a sheet. Was it a stain, anyway, that it should be removed? Any more than she should remove herself—and she was not a stain—from his bed. Yes, he *wanted* her to be there, when it might have been her role, in another life, in a commoner, comic story, to be already scurrying downstairs, still adjusting her clothing. It was his wish, before he left, to see her there, to have her there, nakedly and—who knows?—immovably occupying his bedroom, so that the image of her would be there, branding itself on his mind, even as he met—his vase.

She was doing, as she lay there, the right, the finest thing. She understood it, even as she understood that her lying there had lost all argument, all pleading for his not going. He was clearly going. And he wanted her, for some reason she couldn't fathom, to watch, even as she blazoned her nakedness, this business of his getting dressed, of his putting back on again the life that was his.

Why was he being so slow?

The room had been filled now with as much light and unseasonal warmth as was possible. The minute hand on his watch must be moving towards one, even beyond it. The dark line on the sundial in the garden at Beechwood—where she might have been sitting right now, a book on her lap—would have crept further round. She could not make out the face of the little clock on the dressing table—the two brothers, either side, guarding it.

Was there ever such a day as this? Could there ever be such a day again?

IT WOULD BE Ethel's job, she realised, to deal with the stain—the trickle, the patch. Ethel who would even now, she imagined, be sitting in a house filled with the pricey smell of roasting beef—on such a warm day, when a bit of cold ham might have served. Sitting where her mother had commanded her to sit and not get up or lift a finger. It was her day off, wasn't it? Today everything was different, special. "Talk to your dad for a while, Ethel." If Ethel still had a dad, or a dad still in one piece. For these few hours of reunion, of mother-honouring, Ethel's mother would toil in the kitchen and Ethel's mother and father would live for a week on bread and dripping.

But Ethel when she returned to her duties later—when "the shower" would have perhaps also returned, invigorated yet fatigued from

their sunny outing and in need of attention—
would have to change the sheets in Mister Paul's
bedroom, not having been present earlier to do
so, and would notice the stain. In so far as Ethel
noticed such things, since it was her job simul-
taneously to notice them and quickly make it
seem that they had never existed.

Even Ethel, who had sat down only hours ago,
like royalty, to roast meat, would know what
such a stain was. It was the common lot of her
kind to come upon them, in bedrooms. So much
so that they were sometimes known, in below-
stairs parlance, as "come-upons." There were
other expressions, of varying inventiveness,
including "maps of the British Isles." If there
had to be any actual, awkward professional dis
cussion of them, they might be officially known
as "nocturnal emissions"—which did not necessarily cover all circumstances and might not
leave a new maid of sixteen fully enlightened.
Little boys—not so little boys—had nocturnal
emissions that, setting aside the fact that they
might have had them more considerately, had to
be rendered rapidly absent.

All this she had gleaned for herself before

arriving at Beechwood, when she had been briefly dispatched, as part of her "training" and on a sort of probation, to a big house requiring extra staff for the summer occupancy. There had been five maids in all and, my, how some of them had talked.

There were many emissions that were not produced solitarily and were not, directly, emissions at all (or even necessarily nocturnal), and most maids, using their powers of deduction, could tell the difference and, using their powers of deduction further, might even draw conclusions as to exactly how the "emission" had been formed. But this was not in any way to be spoken of or even acknowledged. Though it was one of the things that could make a maid's work interesting. All the stains, all the permutations. A summer house party with twenty-four guests. Oh Lord.

And even Ethel would have her deductions and conclusions, though she would be staunch in pretending she'd never had to have them. And Ethel's conclusion would be that in the period of time in which the house would have been (supposedly) vacated, Mister Paul would have taken the opportunity to entertain his fiancée, Miss Hobday, in his bedroom. For no other reason, possibly, than that they could do such a thing and get away with it. Setting aside that they might have waited. In two weeks' time they would not need to be such pranksters. Setting aside what kind of woman (one did not discuss Mister Paul) it suggested Miss Hobday was.

It was not for her, Ethel, to judge. Further deduction, along with received, whispered knowledge, might have told Ethel that Miss Hobday was at least one kind of woman: Mister Paul had not invited her to Upleigh for the express purpose of deflowering her. But in any case Ethel, already gathering up the sheets for the laundry basket, would assume that Mister Paul, if he'd taken stock of the stain at all, would have known that she, Ethel, would make it vanish, like the good fairy she was.

Except, as it would turn out, the whole situation—the whole atmosphere and needs of the household—would be different. No one, certainly, would be interested, if they ever had been, in whether Ethel had had a good time with her mother. And anyway Ethel would already have changed the sheets.

SHE HAD NEVER watched a man get dressed before. Though she had to deal intimately with men's garments, and during that summer at the big house had been rapidly educated in the astonishing range of them that one man might own and in their complications and intricacies. Though she had often and in a strange variety of places (stables, greenhouse, potting shed, shrubbery) interfered intimately with Paul Sheringham's clothes, even as he was wearing them, on the condition of course—or, rather, assumption—that he could interfere with hers.

He put the shirt on first, the clean white shirt he'd brought from the dressing room. To put it on—or, rather, enter it—he hoisted it above his head, like any woman tunnelling into a shift. She hadn't thought it would be the shirt first. But to every act of gentlemanly dressing there must be a mix of personal preference and prescribed order. In the "old days," after all, a manservant might have "dressed" him. Just as she could still be required to "dress" as well as "undo" Mrs. Niven.

Dressing, anyway, among their kind, was never conceived of as just a flinging on of clothes. It was a solemn piecing together. Though, in the circumstances, he had every reason to be flinging his clothes on as fast as he could. Another man, in another story, might be saying, as he madly tugged and tucked, "Christ, Jay, I have to damn well scoot!"

But his shirt first. That surprised her. Since it meant an immediate loss of dignity, the very thing that in his absence of haste he seemed bent on preserving. It was his trick, she would later think, it was always Paul Sheringham's great trick, to have such scorn for indignity that he never actually underwent it. He had lost his dignity and found it again so many times with her. But any man in just his shirt became automatically comic, and had it been some other story she might well have giggled.

She supposed that there must be two essential choices: the shirt to be tucked into the waiting trousers, or the trousers to receive the waiting shirt. Each might have its advantages. Yet he looked for a moment like a clown or, instead of a man about to face the world (and a fuming fiancée), like an overgrown boy made ready for bed.

Once it would have been so, she thought. A boy in a nightshirt. Once, he had told her— a rare door opening to the past—about Nanny Becky, who'd left when he'd been sent to school. Once, he would have had a nanny to dress and undress him, all three brothers would have had her.

And what a strange thing, a nanny, a substitute mother. Presenting the offspring to their parents at five o'clock, like a cook offering a cake. And where was Nanny Becky now? In some other household presumably. Or at her mother's.

SHE DID NOT giggle at his shirt. It might have been nice to giggle, from her vantage point on the bed. There might have been another world, another life in which all this might have been a regular, casual repertoire. But there wasn't. She might have been some lounging wife in a room in London, watching him dress to be a joke of a lawyer.

They had hardly spoken for some time. A little while ago they'd made gasping, groaning animal noises. It seemed that they'd entered some diminishing gap of existence together in which, to use a phrase only to be known to her in later life, only "body language" might apply. Only her body might speak. She did not want to falsify—or nullify—anything by the folly of putting it into words. And this, in her later life too, would come to be an abiding occupational conundrum.

It seemed that any words they spoke now must be only ruinous banalities. Even as he engaged with the banalities of underpants and socks.

Yet he was putting on his finery. The fresh white shirt. It was a formal shirt. It would require a collar. It was not just a clean soft-collared shirt that might serve for a Sunday outing, a spin in a car with the top down. It was—even then in a rather old-fashioned sense—his "Sunday best."

She watched while he dealt, with unflustered skill, with cufflinks—little silver ovals winking in the sunshine—with collar studs and collar, semi-stiff. He had brought in a tie, a restrained but sheeny thing of slate blue with little white spots. He selected a tie pin. Was that actually, really a tiny diamond? His chin was already smooth—she'd had occasion to feel it—and now anointed with cologne.

It was as if he was dressing for his wedding. But it was not his wedding—yet. He was only going to meet his wife-to-be for a lunch by the River Thames. And if, as now seemed almost certain, he was going to be seriously late, how on earth was being so superbly turned-out going to help?

He had tied his tie studiously, giving due attention to the knot and the hanging lengths before fixing the pin, and all of this still without his trousers on. She did not, could not laugh. Yet it would seem to her later that everything had hinged upon this piece of farcical theatre. Once he put on his trousers all would be lost. If only she had said to him, screamed at him, "Don't put them on!"

But he went now again to the dressing room, lingering there (did he think time had stopped?) for several rustling minutes, then returned, with trousers on, as well as a jacket and shoes, even with a silk handkerchief, exactly complementing his tie, poking from his pocket.

So had it all been because he hadn't decided yet on the trousers—the ones he'd earlier discarded or ones still hanging in the dressing room? She would never know. She would never say, or be able to say, so he could make some quip or elucidate it all, "You took a long time putting on your trousers."

"Ah yes, Jay. So I did."

What a preposterous word anyway: "trousers."

HE STOOD THERE, complete. He gathered the cigarette case and lighter. He needed only, perhaps, a buttonhole. There were the white orchids in the hall. He might actually have been leaving for his wedding. It wasn't today, but he was signalling it anyway, it was perhaps what all this elaborate sprucing was about: he was leaving— wasn't he?—for his marriage. She felt an actual sting of jealousy for the woman who would be the recipient of all this dawdling decking-out. If she wasn't already in a fury of affrontedness.

And *she*, lying here, had had his unwrapped nakedness.

Then it struck her that it might all in fact have been simply for *her. Her* last look. His "going-away" clothes. Surely not. All the same, in spite of herself—they were the first words she'd spoken for some time—she said, "You look very handsome." She tried to make it sound not like some maid's blushing and inappropriate cooing—"Ooo you do look 'andsome, sir"—nor, on the other hand, like some royal approval. "You pass muster, you may go now." She tried to make it not sound even like the steady veiled declaration she wanted it to be.

He did not say to her, "And you look beautiful." He had never said that, never used that word. Only the word "friend." She couldn't even be sure there wasn't some shadow of discomfort in his face at the tribute she'd just paid him.

Only banality would do. Demolish—but do. He delivered a whole speech of it now.

"You don't have to hurry. I don't suppose the

shower will be back till at least four. When you go, lock the front door and put the key under the rock by the boot-scraper. It's not a rock, actually, it's half a stone pineapple. From when Freddy took a swing at it with his cricket bat. But it's what we do, whenever we leave the house empty. Which is hardly ever. And I'm not leaving it empty now, am I? But the shower will expect it—with no Ethel or Iris—if they get back first. It's a whacking great key, they won't have taken it themselves. I'll put it on the hall table. That's all really. Leave everything."

Did he mean by that the sheets, his shirt, his rejected trousers, dangling over the chair? What else could he mean? Was he telling her not to be a bloody maid? All this while he fingered the knot of his tie and tweaked at his cuffs.

"If you're hungry, there's a veal-and-ham pie, or half of one, in the kitchen. I can always tell Cookie I scoffed it. I mean—as well as going out to lunch. Not that I have to tell anyone anything. Anything."

It was his last, oddly echoing remark. Was it just about the veal-and-ham pie?

And later she would chew over not just a

veal-and-ham pie but almost every word of that matter-of-fact speech. It would stay eerily imprinted. But, precisely because of that, it would sometimes seem that she had made it up, that he could not have said all those things that she remembered so clearly, even fifty years later. He might have just said after all, "You'd better get some clothes on, you'd better make yourself scarce."

She would brood over it like some passage that perhaps needed redrafting, that might not yet have arrived at its proper meaning.

Then he was gone. No goodbye. No silly kiss. Just one last look. Like a draining of her, like a drinking up. And what he'd just bestowed on her: his whole house. He was leaving it to her. It was hers, for her amusement. She might ransack it if she wished. All hers. And what was a maid to do with her time, released for the day on Mothering Sunday, when she had no home to go to?

SHE LISTENED to his steps receding down the staircase. They became louder again as they clicked and loitered on the tiles of the hall. He was gathering an item or two before his actual departure? A hat? The buttonhole? Why not? Perhaps he kept a pin for such a thing in his jacket pocket. He was finding that key?

She did not move. She froze. She heard the front door—or doors—being opened, then closed. It was neither a slam nor a gentle manipulation. Then she heard—it came up from outside through the open window, not echoing through the house itself—his sudden giggle. If giggle it was. It was more like some trumpeting, defiant call, weird and startling as a peacock's. She would never forget it.

There was the crunch of his shoes on the gravel. He was walking towards the old stable and his garaged car. He would see her bicycle against the front wall. She'd simply propped it there, since he'd said the front door—and the front door had already been opening magically. She hadn't left it discreetly out of sight. And so, she realised now, if Miss Hobday had decided to turn up mischievously, as a fiancée might in this modern age, in her own car, to surprise him—and surprise him she would have done—she would have seen it: a woman's bicycle, without a crossbar. And then there might have been a scene, a wild and frantic scene. And the day would have turned out very differently.

But wasn't there going to be a scene now in any case, at the Swan at Bollingford?

All the scenes. All the scenes that never occur, but wait in the wings of possibility. It was perhaps already almost half past one. Birds chorused. Somewhere on a road the other side of Bollingford, Emma Hobday, in her Emmamobile, would already be nearing the place of their rendezvous. Or perhaps she too was late. It was her woman's right. Perhaps she was always maddeningly late and perhaps he was only banking on this exasperating habit. If he timed it right they might serenely coincide.

Perhaps that was the simple explanation.

But in any case Emma Hobday would be enjoying, as she drove, the dazzling rush of this spring day. What it might be like to drive a car was beyond her maid's experience—she had only driven a bicycle. But she tried to put herself momentarily in the shoes—or on the wheels—of Emma Hobday who did not know yet what a show of himself her husband-to-be had prepared for her. Or that he'd taken so long in putting on his trousers.

And at Henley they might have finished the smoked salmon and be anticipating perhaps the duck or the lamb with mint sauce—surely not as good as Milly's. And remarking yet again on the marvellous weather, and if only it would repeat itself for the wedding. She imagined a dining room with tall French windows flung open to the sunshine. A lawn leading down to the river. Tables even, laid up, outside. White hats. Like a wedding itself.

All the scenes. To imagine them was only to imagine the possible, even to predict the actual. But it was also to conjure the non-existent.

She heard the car start. A throaty revving or two. Perhaps he always did it, as if a race was starting. And he would surely have to race now, to redeem himself even partially. But she heard the wheels simply crackle, not spin or lurch, over the gravel, then the sound of the engine gathering speed and noise, as he drove between the lime trees and the two big lawns, then getting fainter and simply merging with the birdsong.

She did not move. She did not go to the window. A brief, flourishing roar, as he turned onto the metalled road—the same road he had taken this morning, in the other car, with the honoured but cowed Ethel and Iris—and at last put his foot down.

She didn't move. The curtains stirred slightly. A naked girl in his room. She didn't move—she didn't know how long she didn't move—until it seemed the absurdity of her not moving won out against some dreadful need not to.

Then she moved. She reared up from the pillow. Her feet found the carpet. She walked over it, naked, as he had. The two brothers in their silver frames stared at her. She saw herself in the mirror. She went to the window. There was nothing to see. Berkshire. There was no one to notice her sudden unaccountable face at the window, her bare sunlit breasts. The sky was an unbroken blue.

She turned back into the room, resisting the fleeting urge to begin picking up clothes. She looked at the bed where they had both been, the covers flung back, the dented sheets, the little blatant stain.

She thought of Ethel.

All the emissions. Ethel, maid in a house of boys, would be not unfamiliar with them, though this little stain would be curiously different. All the emissions of three brothers, and two of them gone now. Though there they were, in their silver frames, eyeing a naked girl. And Ethel, she strongly supposed, had never known what it was like to be the direct cause of a man's emission, let alone to feel it inside her, or, mingling with her own fluids, trickling out of her. A maid—and, yes, a maid. And Ethel must be nearing thirty. Her parents must be ancient. But at least she had them and had been allowed to see them today.

All the wasted emissions. The sunlight for a moment seemed to be filling the room only with a bright bare emptiness. But why should she be feeling so bereft and alone in the world when she'd had what she'd had this day? And when, after all, she wasn't Ethel. And when she had right now a whole house along with a small parkland at her disposal—as Mr. Niven might have put it.

SHE WALKED OUT, past the dressing room, into the nearby bathroom. A little masculine temple. She looked at razors and brushes and bottles of cologne and wondered whether to touch them. She wondered whether to touch and finger every last item on the glass shelves. She washed and dried herself anyway, using the basin and the towel—damp from his own use of it—that Ethel would remove unthinkingly.

She'd put in the cap that he'd helped her get. It was why there had been so much dribble. She couldn't have got such a thing without him, and it had all been done, with his usual scorning of difficulty or embarrassment, one day when she'd had the afternoon off. She'd got the 1:20 to Reading and met him. Afterwards, they'd gone to a cinema.

God knows how he'd arranged it. He out-clevered her, perhaps, at some things. "There's a doctor chappie I know, Jay . . ." It had taken her some time to——adapt to it. It was her (their) precious means of prevention.

And suppose, she would think later, she *had* become pregnant. Would she have suffered all the consequences——they would have been all *her* consequences and would have included swift banishment——so that his marriage would not have been cancelled? Would she have borne all that for him?

Suppose she had deliberately neglected to put the thing in, say three months ago.

Suppose.

"A Dutch cap, Jay. So my seed doesn't get anywhere near you. I mean, any nearer than it needs to."

She didn't know what was Dutch about it. But part of her maid's outfit was a little white cap. So there were times when she was wearing two caps.

And "seed." That was another strange word, or it was a strange way of using it, since it didn't look like anything resembling seed——the pips in an apple, the tiny black things that might dust a loaf. And yet it was the proper and the right word, she could see that too, and she rather liked it. And it was the word he'd first used for it, when she first became acquainted with the stuff. "It's my seed, Jay." It seemed so long ago now. "It's my seed. We could put it in the ground and water it and see what happens." She honestly hadn't known if he was being serious.

And now it was springtime. Seed time. "We plough the fields and scatter . . ."

All the emissions.

Had her mother been a pregnant maid? Was that the whole story? Had her mother not had a cap to put in? All the omissions. As Milly might have put it.

SHE WENT INTO the dressing room. She was tempted to touch, finger—even try on—everything that hung in it. It was something that servants could only wonder at. What will it be today? Who shall I be today? How had he chosen, on such a day, his almost severe yet perfect steel-grey jacket?

She went back into the bedroom. There was the soft onslaught of the birdsong again. The far-off snorting of a train.

She might retrieve her clothes, put them on and leave at once. What was the phrase she had sometimes read in books? "Cover her tracks." But he'd said what he'd said: the house was hers. She would truly make it so. And it would have seemed somehow like a wrongness, a retreat, to put her clothes back on again.

She went out onto the landing, into shadow, her bare feet on mossy carpet. Shafts and dapples of sunlight from some upper window or skylight caught the red and brown weaves beneath her, the worn patch at the top of the staircase, the gleam of banisters, the glitter of dust in the air. There was always dust in the air. Why else the need for dusting?

She descended the stairs, her fingers stroking the rail more out of delicate assessment than to steady herself. Where the stairs turned, stair rods gleamed. Ethel was no slouch. Below, the hall seemed to tense at her approach. Objects might have scuttled and retreated. They had never witnessed anything like this before. A naked woman coming down the stairs!

Her feet struck the coolness of the hall tiles. On one side of the exit to the vestibule was a grandfather clock, on the other a full-length mirror. Across the hall was a table with the large bowl and the sprigs of white flowers. His mother's precious orchids. They did not look like any other flower. They had a stillness, an insistence, each little bloom was like a frozen butterfly.

Might he have picked one before he left? They looked indeed too precious to be picked. But what should he care? It was not his way to respect such things. As it was not his way, plainly, to respect punctuality. The grandfather clock said a quarter to two! And who would notice one little flower missing from the stem? If there was one missing now, she wasn't noticing it.

It was all in her head, in any case, that he might have picked an orchid. Then stood before the mirror to attach it. As was the picture that she might have stood here and picked one for him. "Here—before you go." And held it to his lapel.

Pictures hung around the hall, as they hung, in step-fashion themselves, above the stairs, as they hung also around the walls at Beechwood. It was a strange thing, this need among their kind for pictures to adorn the walls, since she had never seen Mr. or Mrs. Niven actually stand before a picture and look at it. They were things, perhaps, only to be noted out of the corner of the eye, or only for visitors to appreciate. Or rather for maids to study closely and be their true connoisseurs, as they dusted the frames and cleaned the glass.

She had stared repeatedly at all the pictures at Beechwood, so that she would remember them always, even when she was ninety, like some thumbed catalogue in her head, as people apparently remembered with uncanny clarity the illustrations in their first children's books. As she would remember always the big gloomy pictures of men in dark coats—benefactors, overseers—that hung in the hall in the orphanage, where there had been no reading of bedtime stories.

Could she "catalogue" this place? Or at least

take in and preserve in some way its sudden crowding presence for her, its multiplicity of contents. Given that she would never be here again. Given that she could only give it so long—how long might she dare?

And how long before, for him, the catalogue of this place, in his new life, might seep from his head? Not quickly, she imagined, even hoped. And how long before, for him, the catalogue of all the moments with her . . . ? Before even this day would fade.

WITHIN THE VESTIBULE—it was much like at Beechwood—there were all the regular accompaniments—umbrella stand, hat stand—of departures and arrivals, gatherings or sheddings of coats. Here (though it was Ethel's task) she might easily have stood to practise that essential art of the servant of being both invisible yet indispensably at hand. She was invisible now.

On a little felt-topped narrow table where gloves and other belongings might sometimes rest she saw the key that he'd left out for her. It was large and very key-like and somehow like some troubling, waiting test, though it was not the key for opening anything, merely for locking up.

She did not want to touch it yet.

She turned back into the hall, where a choice of doors and directions faced her. It did not matter perhaps. She had no particular business in any of the rooms—except the bedroom upstairs, where the business was over. Yet her general and compelling business seemed to be to impregnate with her unseen, unclothed intrusion this house that was and wasn't hers.

And so she did. She glided from room to room. She looked, took in, but also secretly bestowed. She seemed to float on the knowledge that, outrageous as her visiting was—she hadn't a stitch on!—no one would know, guess she had even been here. As if her nakedness conferred on her not just invisibility but an exemption from fact.

Ethel would know of course. But Ethel would think she had been Miss Hobday.

She entered the drawing room. It was like a small deserted foreign country, a collection of pleading but abandoned possessions. As if life itself—she had never had this thought at

Beechwood—was the sum of its possessions. She could not help entering it with the studied deference of a maid announcing a caller or bringing in tea. Yet there was no one there. It was almost like entering those unalterable shrines of the boys' rooms at Beechwood—no need to knock but you felt you should—and she decided at once that she wouldn't go into the equivalent rooms that must be here upstairs. Had she really thought she would? Like this?

The gilt mirror over the mantelpiece suddenly leapt to arrest her, to prove her undeniable, flagrant presence. Look, this is you! You are here!

And had he supposed that *he* was exempt from fact? That a quarter past two might conveniently turn into half past one? She tried to guess the exact calibration of minutes by which his lateness would be merely excused, excused but with frostiness, excused but with hot anger, not excused at all. Not excused, even with the forgiving closeness of their wedding—not excused especially because of that.

She tried to put herself again in the shoes, the skin of Emma Hobday. On the mantelpiece was an invitation, on thick, gold-edged, round-cornered card, expensively printed with scrolling black letters. It was an invitation to Mr. and Mrs. Sheringham from Mr. Hobday and Mrs. Hobday to the wedding of their daughter, Emma Carrington Hobday. It was a formality of course, and had been put there on the mantelpiece simply in proud proclamation. As if they would not have gone to their son's wedding.

"Carrington"?

Returning to the hall, she went to stand before the tall mirror, as though to put herself in her own oddly intangible skin. She had never before had the luxury of so many mirrors. She had never before had the means to view her whole unclad self. All she had in her maid's room was a little square of a mirror, no bigger than one of the hall tiles.

This is Jane Fairchild! This is me!

Paul Sheringham had seen, known, explored this body better than she had done herself. He had "possessed" it. That was another word. He had possessed her body—her body being almost all she possessed. And could it be said that she had possessed and might always possess him?

And had he ever "possessed" Emma Hobday? Well, he would in two weeks.

She tried to picture Emma Hobday's naked body—how it might resemble or not resemble hers. But she couldn't. She couldn't even imagine Emma Hobday without clothes. What was she wearing now, on a March day that was like June? A flowery summer frock? A straw hat? She tried to see Emma Hobday in the mirror. It was even hard to see—though he must have stood before this mirror, a last magnificent look, orchid or no orchid, less than an hour ago—*him*.

Can a mirror keep a print? Can you look into a mirror and see someone else? Can you step through a mirror and *be* someone else?

The grandfather clock chimed two o'clock.

She had not known he was already dead.

SHE TURNED, to consider another choice of doors, and, opening one and then another, found herself in the library. It was not, perhaps, such a random choice. Houses have patterns and proper "houses," even modest ones like Beechwood or

Upleigh, had their libraries. In any case she was glad it was where she found herself to be.

Libraries too—libraries especially—had normally to be entered with much delicate knocking and caution, though as often as not, judging by the one at Beechwood, there was actually no one inside. Yet even when empty they could convey the frowning implication that you should not be there. But then a maid had to dust—and, my, how books could gather dust. Going into the library at Beechwood could be a little like going into the boys' rooms upstairs, and the point of libraries, she sometimes thought, was not the books themselves but that they preserved this hallowed atmosphere of not-to-be-disturbed male sanctuary.

So, few things could be more shocking than for a woman to enter a library naked. The very idea.

The Beechwood library had its wall's worth of books, most of which (a maid knows) had hardly ever been touched. But in one corner, near a buttoned-leather sofa, was a revolving bookcase (she liked to twirl it idly when she was cleaning) in which were kept books that clearly had been read. Surprisingly perhaps, in such a generally grown-up place, they were books that harked back to childhood, boyhood or gathering manhood, books that she imagined might once have flitted between the library and those silent rooms upstairs. There were even a few books that looked newly and hopefully purchased, but never actually begun.

Rider Haggard, G.A. Henty, R.M. Ballantyne, Stevenson, Kipling ... She had good reason to remember the names and even the titles on some of the books. *The Black Arrow*, *The Coral Island*, *King Solomon's Mines* ... She would always see their grubby, frayed dust jackets or the exact coloration of their cloth bindings, the wrinklings and fadings of their spines.

Of all the rooms at Beechwood, in fact, the library, for all its dauntingness, was the one she most liked to clean. It was the room in which she most felt like some welcome, innocent thief.

ONE DAY, after she had lodged her bold but shy, even slightly simpering request, Mr. Niven had said, after a lengthy pause for thought, "Well yes, of course you may, Jane." The pause might have suggested that he was permitting some inversion in the hierarchy of the household, or just his puzzlement on a practical point: Well when was she going to read the things, with all her duties to perform? In her sleep? It might have suggested amazement—had the ability not long ago been put to the test—that she could read at all.

But it was nonetheless a yielding, even kindly pause.

"Of course you may, Jane."

They were magic, door-opening words. A different answer—"Who do you think you are, Jane?"—might have undone her life.

It deserved one of her full bobbings. Nothing less.

"But you must let me know which book first. And, of course, you must return it."

"Of course, sir. Thank you very much, sir."

She became a borrower from the Beechwood library, on a carefully monitored yet intrigued, even fostered basis. In fact things took a noticeably sensitive turn with Mr. Niven when it became clear which section of the library she was really interested in. She wouldn't have wanted, after all, to read Foxe's *Book of Martyrs* or Smiles's *Lives of the Engineers* (in five volumes). Who would?

"*Treasure Island*, Jane? What do you want to read *Treasure Island* for? All these books for boys."

It wasn't really a question or query at all, but more like some general bafflement—or a sort of being caught off his guard. He might perhaps have said, with a lot of coughing, "Not those books, Jane. Any books but those."

As for his other observation, well where were the books for girls?

Which she didn't mind at all. Boys' stuff, adventure stuff. She didn't mind not reading girls' stuff, whatever that might be. Adventure. The word itself often loomed and beckoned from the pages: "adventure."

It did not seem that the Nivens of Beechwood, or their kind generally, though they had time and means, were in any way adventurous or even advocates of the idea of adventure. "A jamboree in Henley." Libraries themselves were like dry, sober rejections of adventure. Yet in the Beechwood library was this little spinning cache of stuff that had once, plainly, been gulped down, like an allowable dosage before the onset of tedious or terrible maturity.

Mr. Niven might have said, "Not that bookcase please, Jane." But he didn't.

AND LATER, much later in her life, she would say in interviews, in answer to a perennial (and tedious) question, "Oh, boys' books, adventure books, they were the thing. Who would want to read sloppy girls' stuff?"

Her eyes might glint, her wrinkled face purse up a bit more. But then she might say, if she wanted to be less skittish, that reading those books then—"the war, you understand, the first one that is, was barely over"—was like reading across a divide. So close, yet a great divide. Pirates and knights-in-armour, buried treasure and sailing ships. But they were the books she had read.

THE LIBRARY AT Upleigh was remarkably similar. There was the same dominant wall of books that looked as though they had never been read. There were the same small white or black busts—as if from a central warehouse—of men with heavy brows and beards and toga-draped shoulders. There was a desk and, instead of the leather sofa, two dumpy red-brick-coloured armchairs. There was a rack of newspapers and magazines, strange objects of modernity in what might have been a museum. Sunlight came from the window between half-drawn curtains and stretched itself in a bright rectangle over the soft-brown carpet.

On the desk was a small stack of what she recognised as law books. But it was the only sign— it even looked rather arranged—of his supposed intentions while the house was empty and at peace. On a morning like this? Mugging up. She imagined anyway that his diligent studying would have consisted of putting his feet up on the desk and smoking several cigarettes.

She seemed to see him actually doing this, like a ghost in the room. That made two ghosts then. But her ghost was—had been—palpably and unadornedly there. Though no one would ever know.

It was only March, but such was the warmth

that a fly was buzzing and knocking obstinately against the window. And then she saw it, on the other side of the desk: a little enclave of books very similar to the one she knew and had recourse to at Beechwood. She even recognised familiar titles, books she had actually read. So she was not a stranger or trespasser here. In some way she even belonged.

But if Paul Sheringham had ever gone near any of these books, he never said. He gave the impression that he thought there were many things at Upleigh that ought by now to have been chucked away. After all, the bloody horses had all gone. And when she'd told him about her own reading at Beechwood (she wished she hadn't) he'd scoffed, as he scoffed at so many things, and said, "All that tommyrot, Jay? You read all that stuff?" And reminded her at once that their relationship was essentially bodily, physical and here-and-now, it wasn't for droning on about books.

A lawyer? Hardly.

The only difference at Upleigh was that the "boys' books" were not in a separate bookcase, revolving or otherwise, but in a little section (perhaps once cleared of weightier matter) of the main big case, convenient for access.

And the other difference of course was that she was standing naked in the library at Upleigh, something she had never done at Beechwood.

She took one of the books from the shelf in front of her and opened it, and then, for reasons she couldn't have explained, pressed it nursingly to her naked breasts. It was a copy of *Kidnapped*. She knew it. She had read the copy from the bookcase at Beechwood. There was the map of "The Wanderings of David Balfour." There were the words "I will begin the story of my adventures . . ."

She pressed the book to her, then replaced it. No one would know. No one would know about that book's little wandering and adventure. No one would know about the "map" on the sheet upstairs.

SHE LEFT the library. The house's scattered retinue of clocks ticked and whirred. It was the only sound. Outside, the world shone and sang. Here everything was muted, suspended, immured.

She turned into a passage that she instinctively

knew would take her to the stairs to the kitchen. This one, after she descended the stairs, was so still and quiet it might as well have been a library. She felt its unnerving calm. Any kitchen normally has a residual warmth, but this one, beneath the sunny upper floors and left inert all morning, was distinctly cool. But that was her fault perhaps, for wearing no clothes.

Goose bumps emerged on her skin. So too did a vulgar gurgle from her stomach.

The pie, with a knife for cutting it, was on the table, beneath a blue-and-white tea towel. Beside it was a tray with cutlery, napkin, condiments, a bottle of beer and a glass, a bottle opener. The whole collation was presented so that Mister Paul might carry it up to any part of the house if he cared to—the library, for example, so as not to interrupt his studies. That is, if he did not wish to savour the novel experience of eating by himself in the kitchen—and assuming, of course, that he didn't have other plans for passing his time and taking his luncheon.

Who anyway, on a day like this, would really want to bury their nose in a book?

It was a half-pie, a leftover, but, even so, too

much for one. But she attacked it with a sudden ravenous unmannerly hunger. There was no one to watch. He might have done this, she supposed, if the day had turned out differently, if it had followed the course of the pretence he'd invented for it. He might have come down to the kitchen and, suddenly relishing the perverse pleasure of it, wolfed the pie right there at the table. He might have ceased to be the aloof and splendid Paul Sheringham and, with no one to see, become, cheeks bulging, like some guzzling schoolboy or starving tramp.

And she, in her ladylike liberty—and with two and six in her pocket—might have stopped at some village tea shop for egg-and-cress sandwiches and cake.

He must by now be sitting down in his impeccable get-up, with her, at the Swan. Though how might he have accomplished that? By magic? By sheer gall and bravado? "Well, I'm here now . . ." Or readiness to stake everything? "Well, if you want to call it off . . ."

Had that even been his brutal, polished plan? It gave her a brief tingle of hope. To call it off—first clearing his path by causing serious displeasure.

She tried anyway to imagine the scene, even as she chewed on the pie, as he himself, sitting here, might have chewed on it: cheeks crammed, pieces spilling. She wanted to eat this pie, which he hadn't eaten, for him. As if she *were* him.

It was a very good pie. She opened the bottle of beer and drank, if only to wash down the food. It tasted as beer had always tasted the few times she'd drunk it, like brown autumn leaves. She attacked the pie again. Then she felt suddenly like the most miserable and desperate of creatures: no clothes to her back, no roof of her own, and eating someone else's pie.

She shivered. She got to her feet. The pie was too much anyway. She burped loudly. She left everything as it was. She left it, she thought, only as he would have left it—as he had left his discarded clothes. She even turned at the door to see it as if it were all his heedless doing. Ethel would clear it up, of course, later. Ethel or Iris. And it was strange, either of them might think, that he'd eaten the pie, or most of it, if he'd gone to have lunch with Miss Hobday. And if he'd gone to have lunch with Miss Hobday then it was strange that there was also that patch on the sheet

But Ethel, if it was for her to note both pie and patch, might piece together a story, not unlike one she herself, the Beechwood maid, had fleetingly envisaged. That Miss Hobday, on such a beautiful morning, had taken it upon herself to drive all the way to Upleigh and "surprise" Mister Paul. Meanwhile Mister Paul, toiling at his law books, had got bored and hungry and remembered the veal-and-ham pie. The marauded but unfinished remnants and the barely broached bottle of beer might indeed suggest he had been surprised in his mid-morning raid of the kitchen. And after Miss Hobday's arrival one thing had, unexpectedly or not, led to another, accounting for the stain on the sheet.

And then Mister Paul and Miss Hobday, having taken advantage of the empty house, had left for their lunch, each driving their own car, to preserve the appearance that they had met at their rendezvous. Ethel might even have remembered Mister Paul's saying, on that strange little drive to the station, that he dared say he'd be meeting Miss Hobday for lunch, and then Iris saying that she'd put out a bit of veal-and-ham pie for him anyway, just in case. He wasn't obliged of course to discuss his plans with the servants, and it was peculiar if he did. But then his personally taking them to the station was rather peculiar too.

It was a peculiar day.

Ethel, she supposed later, might have constructed such a story, and she might even have seen, when the time came, how her story had its failings. But much the greater likelihood was that Ethel, when attending to one or both messes, would not have thought very much about either of them, or their nefarious implications, it not being her business to think about such things. She had enough to think about anyway, having just been to her mother's.

Would Ethel even have thought, or would Iris, who had much more to do with the pie: Well if he ate the pie, it was the last meal he ate?

SHE ASCENDED the stairs. There was another kind of popular book besides the boys' adventure book and one even favoured by adults. But she would say, in her interviews, that she had never had much time for the detective story. For reading them—let alone writing them. Life itself was riddle enough.

She climbed up from the kitchen into the warmth and light of the upper floors. And now, though she had no actual need to hurry—the clock in the hall said twenty past two and the world was still at lunch—she wished to leave, she had explored sufficiently.

It was then anyway (so she would always know the exact timing of its ringing) that the telephone—or a telephone—rang from some nearby recess she hadn't previously noticed. She froze. She had the odd sensation that it had rung because she'd moved close to it. She didn't answer it anyway, it would have been foolish to answer it, though she was quite good at answering telephones. Its ringing went on for some time while she stood stock-still, as if, had she moved, the telephone might somehow have observed her, which was foolish too.

But wasn't it utterly foolish anyway to be standing here in this unfamiliar hall with nothing on?

She climbed the staircase and re-entered the bedroom. It was the same, of course it was, as she had left it. Only the sun, still flooding in, had lowered its angle a little. There was the open window, the clothes over the armchair, his unwanted trousers, still scarfed with one of her stockings. The pulled-back bedclothes. The patch, a little drier. Yet it seemed like a room round which, even in such a short interval, some invisible fence had been raised. Was it really the room in which . . . ? Was it really here that . . . ?

It was the profoundest of questions. Had it really happened?

Beyond the window the birds chirped eternally and in the blue sky she could not see, or would not remember seeing, any flaw.

The mirror on the dressing table offered its last three-fold glimpse of her nakedness. She put on her clothes. They slipped on like some much-used disguise. She touched—only to touch, to stroke, not to tidy—his trousers. She didn't close the open window. Again, as he might have carelessly left it. Ethel's job. And who anyway was going to come with a ladder . . . ? She did not touch the bed, even to cover the patch.

The young men in their frames on the dressing table seemed now oblivious of her. Was it all her vain fancy that they had previously peeped? They looked immovably through her, at some camera that had clicked long ago. She stood in the doorway and took her own last mental photograph. Then left.

In the hall she paused again and took— plucked—one of the orchid flowers from the clusters above the bowl. Well, if he hadn't, she would. She realised at once that it would be the most incriminating of items, if she were to wear it. If she were to return to Beechwood with an orchid stuck in her frock. But it wasn't for wearing. She slipped it where earlier in the day she had slipped her half-crown. It would get quickly bruised and tattered perhaps, but it was her proof to herself. It was so she herself would always know. No one else ever would.

ADVENTURE STORIES, not detective stories. Boys' books. They were the thing. And her interviewer might say, treating it all as a bit of a joke and not anyway wanting the interview to get too "booky": "And boys themselves?"

"Oh yes," she would say with an away-with-you flip of her eighty-year-old hand, as if there had once been queues. The audience in their darkened seats might titter obligingly. And the interviewer might not even see, amid the playfulness, the brief narrowing of the eyes at the change of subject.

It was that life itself might be an adventure. That was the submerged message (the "subtext" they might say now) of all those books. Was there in fact any other way to live? And adventure did not have to be about pirates and narrow escapes. It might be a constant mental hazarding. Suppose, imagine. Imagine. What did writers do with their time? They were the most unadventurous souls on earth, weren't they? Sitting all day at their desks.

But she would not say such things in interviews. Only, with her protective twinkle and ironically squeezed lips, skirt teasingly round their intimate truth.

I will begin the story of my adventures . . .

SHE PUT the key under the chunk of stone pineapple. She could not see how Freddy could have broken it with a cricket bat. A battle-axe possibly. And she did not know which one was Freddy in the silver frames. She might have asked, she ought to have asked, but she hadn't. "Which one is which? Tell me about them." Would it have been the moment, lying there together? Or would he have fended off the question, a look on his face of having tasted something bad?

Now she would never know.

There, against the wall, was her bicycle, her potentially incriminating bicycle that had incriminated no one. She steered it for a while across the gravel before mounting, drawing deep unsteady breaths. She was slightly sore where she met the saddle. She tucked and gathered her skirt. The air was warm and bright and brimming round her.

A sudden unexpected freedom flooded her. Her life was beginning, it was not ending, it had not ended. She would never be able to explain (or be required to) this illogical, enveloping inversion. As if the day had turned inside out, as if what she was leaving behind was not enclosed, lost, entombed in a house. It had merged somehow— pouring itself outwards—with the air she was breathing. She would never be able to explain it, and she would not feel it any the less even when she discovered, as she would do, how this day had turned really inside out. Could life be so cruel yet so bounteous at the same time?

She rode off. She did not ride—as he'd departed and she'd arrived—along the drive to the gate and the road. Old habit and old secrecy made her take the old route. Past the stables, through the rhododendrons, past the vegetable plot, the potting shed, the cold frames and greenhouse, then along mere threading paths and through narrow gaps between neglected shrubs into a jumbled outer region that led to a copse. Every twist and turn, every screening outbuilding and clump of vegetation was familiar to her. They had met among them and made use of them often enough. It was even his standard directive: "the garden path."

The secret back route from Beechwood to Upleigh would remain always in her head, such that she might at any time have easily drawn its map, like the map in *Treasure Island* or of David Balfour's wanderings in the Highlands. She would retain the ability, but of course it would be a contradiction, a betrayal, actually to draw a secret map.

"The garden path, Jay." And, once, with a strange echoing sincerity, "I won't ever lead you up it."

The copse led to a small wilderness of rough grass and brambles, then a straggly hedgerow, where there was another way out of what was still Upleigh land. It involved lifting the bicycle fully over a stile, but she had done it enough times. She might, of course, have left the bicycle—it was her usual practice—safely hidden in the hedgerow. But his crisp command had simply empowered her. The front door.

Beyond the hedgerow—it was dense and spreading at this point and it seemed that even in the space of hours the hawthorns had sprouted more green leaves and more white frothing blossom—there was the curve of a narrow minor road. Once on its surface, she could speed anywhere, a mere carefree wayfarer, out pedalling on a heavenly Sunday afternoon.

Though for a crippling moment she didn't know which way to turn. It must have been perhaps three o'clock. She had half the afternoon yet. To turn left would have been the quickest way back to Beechwood, so the obvious choice was right. But where to? Pushing off, she decided that it didn't matter, the main thing was simply to be riding, careering through this warm exhilarating air, and since the road to the right took her down a long sunny swoop then up a gentle rise (it was the back of the Upleigh grounds) her decision, to be indecisive, was confirmed.

Pedalling hard at first, then freewheeling and gathering speed, she heard the whirr of the wheels, felt the air fill her hair, her clothes and almost, it seemed, the veins inside her. Her veins sang, and she herself might have sung, if the rushing air had not stopped her mouth. She would never be able to explain the sheer liberty, the racing sense of possibility she felt. All over the country, maids and cooks and nannies had been "freed" for the day, but was any of them— was even Paul Sheringham—as untethered as she?

Could she have done what she'd done today

if she'd had a mother to go to? Could she have had the life she didn't yet know she was going to have? Could her mother have known, making her dreadful choice, how she had blessed her?

And, like a mother to herself, she would never forget that girl on a bicycle, though she would never mention her to anyone, never breathe a word.

Girl? She was twenty-two. The air up her skirt and a Dutch cap up her fanny.

BEYOND THE TOP of the rise was a crossroads with one of those four-fingered country sign-posts, black on white. She might have taken any direction and ridden off for ever. She had her hidden treasure. She had taken a secret munch of pie and swig of ale in that house over there, behind the trees!

But she stopped for a long time at the cross-roads. Three o'clock. At Henley now, puddings finished, they might be reflecting on the forth-coming event. Mr. Hobday would have estab-lished his benign authority over the assembly and Mr. Niven might have become hopeful that he would not have to share the bill. Meanwhile at Bollingford the subjects of their rosy considerations might have passed miraculously—who knows?— beyond the moment of almost terminal conflagration. Fireworks quenched by champagne. Emma Hobday might have succumbed to Paul Sheringham's impregnable poise. "Must we, Emsie? On a day like this? Just because I was half an hour late . . . All right, forty minutes. What's ten minutes?" His hand, by now, finding her knee.

Is that how it might have gone after all? All the scenes. Suppose.

She stood, one foot on the verge, the other on a pedal. There was not a murmur, in any direction, of traffic. There was only the birdsong and, in the warm air, the half-heard stirring and rousing of—everything. Spring.

She took the left turn, only, after a mile or so, to take another left turn. It was a circuitous way back to Beechwood. She had still half the afternoon, yet she knew, now, what she wanted to do with her remaining time.

It was what she might have done anyway, what she might have said to Mr. Niven, had not circumstances happily dictated otherwise. Or she might have just set off on this bicycle, with a sandwich from Milly and two and six, and found some sunny quiet spot. To sit, to lie, with her bicycle and her book. It was a book by Joseph Conrad. She'd never heard of him. She'd only just begun it.

She might have brought the book with her, she thought, so she might have had it now. But that was absurd. The front door, with her Dutch cap—and a book to read! But she might, all along—had not the telephone triumphantly rung—have said that thing about just sitting in the garden with a book.

"If I may, Mr. Niven."

And he might have said, imagining the rather charming scene, "Of course you may, Jane."

Well, now she would finish her day, her Mothering Sunday, as it might have begun.

And so it was that in order to keep an appointment with a book—with Joseph Conrad—she turned left, then left again, making her way back to Beechwood earlier than needed, though, even so, not directly or quickly. She might still enjoy this glorious sunshine and the thrill of being so fully alive in it, on a whirring, whizzing bicycle. She might still stamp the memory of it on herself for ever.

And so it was that she reached Beechwood some while after four, only to discover that Mr. and Mrs. Niven had, surprisingly, already returned. There was Mr. Niven, as she rode up the drive, standing on the gravel beside the Humber, almost as she had last seen him that morning, though clearly, as she drew near him, in a very different frame of mind. And saying, "Jane. Is that you, Jane?"

What a strange thing to say. Was she someone else?

"Jane, is that you—back so early? I have some distressing news."

ONE DAY, when it had long been her business— her profession, even the reason why she was "well known"—to write stories and to deal intricately with words, she would be asked another perennial and somewhat tedious question: "So when—so how did you become a writer?" She had answered it enough times and, really, you couldn't answer it in a different way every time. Yet people—surprisingly since her occupation was telling stories—did not jump to the conclusion that in giving her standard answer, she might also be telling a story, only kidding, as it were. They took her at her word. And, after all, it was a good answer, a fairly unchallengeable one.

"At birth. At birth, of course," she would say, even when she was asked this question in her seventies or eighties or nineties, when her birth, always a mysterious fact, now seemed the remotest and strangest of events.

"I was an orphan," she would divulge for the umpteenth time. "I never knew my father or mother. Or even my real name. If I ever had one. That has always seemed to me the perfect basis for becoming a writer—particularly a writer of fiction. To have no credentials at all. To be given a clean sheet, or rather, to *be* a clean sheet yourself. A nobody. How can you become a somebody without first being a nobody?"

And a characteristic glint might enter her eye, an additional crease appear at the corner of her mouth, and her interviewer might think that, yes, there was a touch of slyness here. Jane Fairchild was known for being a crafty old bird. But the gaze, for all the glinting, was steady, the face, for all its knottiness, essentially straight. It even seemed to be putting the innocent counter-question: You think I would tell you a lie?

"Not just an orphan," she might go on, "but a foundling. Now there's a word for you. Not such a common one, is it, these days? Foundling. It sounds like a word from the eighteenth century. Or from a fairy tale. But I was left on the steps of an orphanage—in some sort of bundle, I suppose—and taken in. That is what I was told. There were places in those days where that sort of thing could happen. 1901. It was a differ-ent world. Not the start in life any of us might wish for. But then in some ways"—the glint would appear again—"the perfect one.

"My name, Fairchild, was one of the names

that were given to foundling children. There were lots of Fairchilds, Goodchilds, Goodbodys and so on who came out of orphanages—so that they would have, I suppose, a well-intentioned start in life. People sometimes ask me—goodness knows why—do I write under my own name, my real name? Well yes I do—it was my given name. Jane Fairchild. But it might as well be a pen name. I might as well call myself Jane Foundling. In fact, it has a rather pleasing ring, don't you think?"

"And the Jane?"

"Oh Jane is just any old girl's name, isn't it? Young girl's, I mean. Jane Austen, Jane Eyre, Jane Russell . . ."

And so, with a gleam in her eye and a tightening of her lips, she would suggest she had come into the world with an innate licence to invent. And with an intimate concern for how words attach to things.

"My birthright, so to speak. If you'll pardon the pun."

But she would never disclose that when she really became a writer, or had the seed of it truly planted in her (and that was an interesting word, "seed") was one very warm day in March, when she was twenty-two and she had wandered round a house without a shred on——naked, you might say, as on the day she was born——and had felt both more herself, more Jane Fairchild, than she'd ever felt before, yet also, as never before, like some visiting ghost. Had felt, you might say, what it truly means to be put down in this world, placed, so to speak, on its extraordinary doorstep.

And how, after all, could you admit to such things in a public interview (sprightly as some of her interviews could be): I wandered naked round a house that wasn't even mine, that I'd never even entered before. And how did I get to be doing that? Well there was a whole story there, a story she'd sworn to herself never to tell. Nor had she. Nor would she.

Though here she was, look, a storyteller by trade.

IT WAS Mothering Sunday 1924. A different thing from the nonsense they call Mother's Day now. And she had no mother, you see.

She was raised in an orphanage, then put into service. Another phrase you don't hear often these days, but another "start in life" she would recommend to the would-be writer (though it was hardly to be recommended in 1980 or 1990). Since it made you an occupational observer of life, it put you on the outside looking in. Since those who served served, and those who were being served—lived. Though sometimes, to be honest, it felt at the time entirely the other way round. It was the servants who lived, and a hard life they had of it, and the ones who were served who seemed not to know exactly what to do with their lives. Proper lost souls, in fact, some of them . . .

She'd been put into service at fourteen. Two years later, in 1917, she'd gone to Beechwood House in Berkshire. She'd been "taken in" once again, you might say, by Mr. and Mrs. Niven, whose family had been recently reduced by the loss of two sons, and who required in those hard-pressed wartime years only a novice maid (meaning perhaps simply cheap) in addition to their existing cook.

Out of motives best known to themselves—though not so difficult to fathom perhaps—they had considered and chosen an orphan, and then discovered that the poor forlorn thing was not so lacking in spark or gumption at all. It turned out she could read, more than many maids could, more than the word "Brasso" on a tin, and could write more than a shopping list, and could do sums.

"Can you tell me, Jane, what are three and six plus seven and six?"

"Eleven shillings, Mr. Niven, sir."

She was half educated.

It even emerged one day that she wanted to read books. Books! And instead of its seeming a damned cheek, it had only stirred further the charitable urges already present in the house. It had only touched some capacity for paternal leniency in Mr. Niven that this orphan girl—this Fairchild—should be allowed to borrow books from his library.

When he learned which kind of book she preferred he might have gently but firmly protested, but perhaps her preference only brought out the leniency all the more. Mr. Niven sometimes disappeared into the library himself. It was what, she sometimes thought, libraries were for: for men to disappear into and be important in, even though they had disappeared. She sometimes thought Mr. Niven went into the library to cry.

The leniency extended to her own occasional "disappearances." Mr. and Mrs. Niven had no complaints about her work generally—the opposite—but she could now and then be oddly absent—beyond, that is, her designated days and half-days off. As when she seemed to take for ever over simple shopping errands. Or those times she said she had a puncture, or her chain had come off again (there seemed to be a curse on the Second Bicycle) and she'd had to seek the kind help of other passing cyclists. But then there were times—true, usually in the quieter stretches of the day—when she was simply not to be found.

Though now perhaps these absences could be explained. She had snatched a moment in her room, not, as once fondly supposed, to bemoan in private her sad orphan's lot, but to read a book.

You could hardly allow her to borrow books and then not allow her at least some time to read them. And the house was not any more, let's face it, as in the old days, a firmly governed, a strictly regimented house. Look where regimentation had got the world.

Had Mr. Niven, had either of them, ever wondered, guessed?

OH YES, she would say, the glint in her eye, she was lucky to have been born with nothing to her name. With not even a name, in fact. Or the real date of her birth. So she was not only nameless, but ageless. And her eighty-year-old face would bloom.

The first of May was the date of birth that had been accorded to her, by rough approximation and perhaps because it was a nice date, just as Jane Fairchild was a nice name. Some mothers, apparently, left a little note, inside the bundle, with just a date of birth and a name. Only the first name. The commoner the better. No one ever deposited a Laetitia. And, if you thought about it, the name must have only been a thought anyway. And wasn't any name just a thought? Why was a tree called a tree?

She might even have liked to be called Jane Bundle.

And did it matter if you marked your birthday on the wrong day? If it had really been the 25th of April, though you never knew. The wrong day became the right day. This was the great truth of life, that fact and fiction were always merging, interchanging. And if you were a maid you weren't given much leisure to mark your birthday anyway—if anyone even knew it. You weren't given the day off. And being a maid was a little like being an orphan, since you lived in someone else's house, you didn't have a home of your own to go to.

Except on Mothering Sunday. When you did get the day off, to go home to your family. Which would always put her at a bit of a loss. What to do, what to do with herself on Mothering Sunday? She could hardly go looking for her mother.

Though what would she have done with herself anyway, with her life, if she hadn't been a maid? And she supposed—the furrowed face would bloom again—that it was a very common human predicament. To be at a loss, not to know what to do with yourself.

"MY YEARS AS a maid," she would call them, "my maid's years," never adding, "but not for long my maidenly ones." "My years in service." It was hard to think now of a time when half the world was "in service." She was born in 1901—at least the year must have been right—and she would grow up to become a maid, which anyone might have predicted. But to become a writer— no one could have predicted that. Not even the kindly committee at the orphanage who had re-conceived her as Jane Fairchild, born on the first of May. And, least of all perhaps, her mother.

When she was asked, in the interviews, to describe the atmosphere of those wartime years (meaning, of course, the First War), she would say that it was so long ago now and so like another world that trying to remember it was a bit like—writing a novel. Had she really been alive then? But if she were honest she would add that she'd been not unaware of it, of course—all that accumulated loss and grief. How could anyone be unaware of it? Every week she dusted two rooms where everything was to remain "just as it was." You went in, took a little breath perhaps, and got on with it.

But she had never known them, the boys who'd had those rooms, and what she mainly thought was: A whole room, full of furniture, *each*. And if you had yourself been comprehensively bereaved at birth—and that was her situation, wasn't it?—how could you share in all that stuff, how could you have anything left over for it? The war wasn't her fault, was it? And, yes, you might say she was lucky, not to have a brother or father, let alone, at that age, a husband to think about. And, yes, you might say it was her good luck to have been raised in a good orphanage, they weren't all evil places rife with abuse. Her mother, whoever she was, had perhaps had some discernment.

So she'd received a rudimentary education

when many who had parents didn't. When many who were packed off to the trenches didn't. She'd been put into service at fourteen with a relatively advanced ability to read and write and— free from all family ties—with perhaps more than a usual eagerness for life.

And who wouldn't want to be Jane Fairchild, born on the first of May?

Oh yes—the face would flower again—she was very fortunate to have been born destitute.

"ARE YOU an orchid, Jane?" Cook Milly had said, after first looking at her very closely, not long after she'd arrived, as if to establish precisely what sort of specimen she would have to work with. "Because my mother was an orchid too."

Had she really said it? And if so, had she used that word deliberately and knowingly— knowing that she was using the wrong word, not the right one? There was a look of purest artlessness and candour in Cook Milly's eye. And did it matter if she'd used the wrong word—if the wrong word was a better one? It would have been wrong to point out that she had made a mistake—to expose, at such a moment, Milly's poor grasp of language and lack of education, while asserting her own accomplishment. That is, if it was a mistake.

And if you were an orphan, then perhaps you might turn into an orchid, as Cinderella turned into a princess.

Had she really said it? Or had she herself misheard it? Or invented this little exchange between herself and Milly? Even then? Surely not. The great truth of life. So that one day she might go on to invent a whole character— a minor but colourful character in her novel *Tell Me Again* (she actually thought of calling her Milly Cook)—who was given to using misapprehended words. Who said "cucumbered" when she meant "encumbered." And in fact the real and living Cook Milly became more and more, in the course of those "maid's years" at Beechwood and certainly by the time of that Mothering Sunday, like some cook in a story book, plump and sturdy and red-cheeked, with thick forearms meant for commanding a mixing bowl.

But what had mattered most—and was strangely clear—was that Cook Milly, who was only three years her elder, was implicitly proposing to be her, Jane Fairchild's, mother—her substitute mother—for the duration. And such was the sincerity that flowed out of Milly that she, the new, disoriented maid, could not help but at once implicitly accept this offer. And never disown it, even though it would emerge that she was a good deal sharper than Cook Milly, so that Milly, who did not have an ounce of cleverness or cunning in her, might be seen as the child of the two of them.

Yet she would always wonder if she had really meant to say "orchid." And how much she might have known, guessed all along, about her and Paul Sheringham.

She would call the character, after all, Molly Cook. And the duration—of her adoption, as it were, by Milly—would be seven years, since within six months of that Mothering Sunday Cook Milly, who had always had her eccentricities with words, went more seriously funny in the head and was taken away to some place (she never knew where, if it wasn't her own poor mother's) where women of her station and condition got taken, never to return.

So she was orphaned, you might say, a second time.

And what if orphans really were called orchids? And if the sky was called the ground. And if a tree was called a daffodil. Would it make any difference to the actual nature of things? Or their mystery?

And what if she had not stayed on the bed but had gone down the stairs with him, still naked, her cool feet on the cool chessboard tiles, to take an orchid from the bowl and hold it to his lapel?

"For me. Since we will never meet again."

Like some far-fetched scene in a far-fetched story book.

SHE WOULD BECOME a writer, and because she was a writer, or because it was what had made her become a writer, be constantly beset by the inconstancy of words. A word was not a thing, no. A thing was not a word. But somehow the two—things—became inseparable. Was everything a great fabrication? Words were like an invisible skin, enwrapping the world and giving it reality. Yet you could not say the world would not be there, would not be real if you took away the words. At best it seemed that things might bless the words that distinguished them, and that words might bless everything.

But she would never say these things in interviews.

She would sometimes discuss them—even discuss them in bed—with her husband Donald Campion. She would call him the Great Dissector. And he would call her the Great Vivisector. Now, there was a word. And she would poke her tongue out at him.

"And what other things do you think are necessary for becoming a writer?"

"Well, you have to understand that words are only words, just bits of air . . ."

The crow's feet round her eyes positively dancing.

"OH, ADVENTURE STORIES, of course, boys' stories. In spite of the fact that there was still a war going on and all that boys' stuff had become sheer nonsense. Sheer tommyrot."

"And—boys themselves?"

"You mean—adventures *with* boys . . . ?"

SHE WOULD BECOME a writer. She would live to be ninety-eight. She would live to have seen two world wars and the reigns of four kings and one queen. And very nearly two queens, since she must have been begotten—only just—in the reign of Queen Victoria. "Begotten, then forgotten."

She was ten years old and in an orphanage when a big ship hit an iceberg, making some more orphans. She was twelve years old when a woman threw herself under a king's horse. She had just turned fifteen when she worked for a while, one summer, in a big house—she had never seen such a palace—and learnt all about nocturnal emissions.

She would live to be almost as old as the century and to know she had probably known and seen—and written—enough. She did not mind, she would cheerfully say, if she did not make it to the year 2000. It was a wonder she had made it this far. Her life had "19" written on it and nineteen was a good age to be. Her face would bloom.

Not that it was really so much—the knowing and seeing—even in seventy, eighty, ninety years. "Her maid's years," "her Oxford years," "her London years," "her Donald years." You lived in your own little cranny, didn't you? All those years at a desk! Even her years of so-called fame, of being shunted around the world, being in places she would never have dreamed of being in—they had all gone by in a blur. And then it was "Jane Fairchild at Seventy," "Jane Fairchild at Seventy-five," "Jane Fairchild at Eighty." For heaven's sake! And batting away the same old questions.

But if you counted what she had seen in her mind's eye. Well then . . . All the places, all the scenes. *In the Mind's Eye*: it was the title of her most well-known book. And could she disentangle it, the stuff she'd seen in her mind's eye, from the actual stuff of her own life? Well, of course she bloody well could, she wasn't a fantasist.

And of course she bloody well couldn't. It was the whole point of being a writer, wasn't it, to embrace the stuff of life? It was the whole point of *life* to embrace it.

"HER OXFORD YEARS"! That was a case in point. Yes, she'd gone to Oxford. She could truly say that, but not in the way, of course, some people could say it. Yet she would love to say gaily and freely in interviews, "Oh yes, I was at Oxford . . ." "When I was at Oxford . . ."

Yes, she had gone to Oxford, in October 1924, to work as an assistant in a bookshop, Paxton's Bookshop in Catchpole Lane. And books, she knew by then, were one of the necessities, the rocks of her life.

It was her first job after being a maid and the first big step in life she had taken for herself. Not a big step, you might think, from maid to shop girl, but it had required some initiative and daring, even some writerly skill, in answering the advert. And it had required Mr. Niven's cooperation in writing her a reference. Perhaps he had said that she'd made more use of his own library than he had.

In any case she had got the job. And Mr. Niven must have understood what a big step it was for her and that she was fully determined to take it, since when she left he gave her ten pounds (ten pounds!) with which to set herself up in Oxford. And she had anyway the money she'd saved from her maid's wages (not having a family that had any call on them), not to mention from the occasional half-crowns and florins Mr. Niven would bestow on her.

Mr. Niven had learnt economy, but there were still the vestiges of largesse.

By this time Milly had left and there was a new cook called Winifred, and there would soon be a new maid too. And she, Jane Fairchild, would never know what became of Beechwood or Upleigh. She would never go back. It was almost a superstition. Some things, some places perhaps take up their truer existence in the mind. Even when she had a car—especially when she had a car—she would never go back, even just to drive by, to stop and look and wonder.

She went to Oxford, to work for Mr. Paxton. She was only an assistant in a bookshop, but an able one, increasingly familiar with books and—what perhaps mattered most—very good with customers, who ranged from mere towns-folk to the cream of the university, even professors. It soon became clear to Mr. Paxton that he had acquired an asset. And it became clear soon enough too that the increasing familiarity with books went with an increasing familiarity with the customers.

The fact was that she began to consort, to go out, even to go to bed with some of them, and it wouldn't have been wrong to say that this is what she had hoped, even vaguely foreseen. If she couldn't have "gone to Oxford" in the other sense, then she became intimate with those who had. It might even be said that she moved in university "circles" even more freely and successfully than many—poor swots that they were—who were actually *there*. She could even pass herself off quite convincingly as that rare and frightening creature, a female undergraduate.

"And what are you studying?"

"Studying? Oh no, I'm just a shop girl."

It was remarkable how their eyes might light up.

And later on she might dare to say, "I'm a shop girl, but—I write too."

One day, in the little back office, Mr. Paxton, close observer of all this and committed family man, had said, "I'm going to get a new typewriter, Jane. This thing has seen better days." There was an awkwardly stoical look in his eye as if he might have been talking about himself. The old typewriter was perfectly serviceable.

"Would you like it?" he said.

And that, you might say, was when she really became a writer. The third time. As well as at birth. As well as one fine day in March, when she was a maid.

HER OXFORD DAYS! Her Oxford years! Oh, they were great days. She saw Oxford all right. It was an education. And, to be perfectly honest, she was sometimes in some respects the educator. Even of some of the best brains in the land. How many, in Oxford? Oh, she couldn't remember now. And of course it was in Oxford that she met her husband, Donald Campion. But that was a whole other story. It was funny how you could say even of life itself: That was another story.

"It wasn't the smoothest of marriages, was it? You and Donald Campion?"

"What makes you say that?"

"Well—two minds. Two careers. He was the bright young philosopher, wasn't he?"

She didn't say, "It was a thing of bodies too." Though at eighty she might have got away with it. If the truth be known—but Donald himself had never known it—Donald had reminded her of Paul Sheringham. And she certainly wasn't going to reveal that in an interview.

"You mean there wouldn't have been room for both his books and mine?" But she didn't say that either. She could clam up sometimes just as effectively as she could quip. What a good mask it was, being turned eighty, with a face like a squeezed-out dish mop.

"And—so tragically short." Her interviewer blundered on.

"Donald or the marriage?" But she didn't say that either.

"Yes, it was tragic," she said, with a voice like flint. And didn't say, as she might have done—at eighty she could be oracular: We are all fuel. We are born, and we burn, some of us more quickly than others. There are different kinds of combustion. But not to burn, never to catch fire at all, that would be the sad life, wouldn't it?

But she'd said it anyway, or something like it, in a book somewhere. And if the truth be known, grief at Donald's death, the second grief of her life, was like the end of her own life. She might have jumped on his pyre. Instead of which she became a better and famous writer.

In the Mind's Eye. It wasn't published, it wasn't finished—in some ways, it wasn't even *begun*—till after Donald was taken away from her in the autumn of 1945 by a brain tumour. His bleak joke was that he'd been too brainy. Another was that there'd be no chance now of his breaking any Secrets Act. He had safely survived the war as a code-breaker, and his best work was perhaps still to come. It would all now, she thought—her own bleak joke—be like a work of fiction.

"We had the same quandary, you know, Donald and I. Words and things."

She had toyed with *All in the Mind*. She had even toyed with *Secrets Act*. But fancy publishing a novel called that. *In the Mind's Eye . . . All in the Mind . . .* Either way, it sounded abstract, even rather cerebral. Ha! Twelve years the wife of a philosopher.

In fact it was her most physical, her most carnal, her most downright *sexual* book. She had found a way, at last, of writing about all that *stuff*. And it was her first big success. She was forty-eight, not so old (there are some mercies) for a writer, but too old to be the mother that, for her own reasons, she'd always shied away from being. You might say she was given no good examples in motherhood. Except Milly. Now, with Donald and his blue-grey gaze and his rat-a-tat laugh gone, she wished she'd yielded.

Forty-eight and famous. *In the Mind's Eye*. Some people were shocked and scandalised. It was only 1950. It would look tame in twenty years' time. And she was—to make it worse—a "lady novelist." A lady novelist? Where did they get that phrase from? And where did they think she came from?

Forty-eight and famous and widowed and childless and not yet halfway through her orphaned life.

"I HAVE SOME distressing news."

Even as Mr. Niven spoke, words displayed their fickle ability to fly away from things. Such was his evident struggle to find words and such her recent experience that she thought he'd said "undressing news." I have some undressing news. A mistake that even Milly couldn't have made.

And when, after he'd got more words out, he said, "You have gone very pale, Jane," she had the fleeting thought that it was surely something people only did in books. People only "went pale" or had "faces of thunder" or eyes that "flashed fire" or blood that "ran cold" in books. Books that she had read.

"I'm so sorry, Jane, to be telling you this. On Mothering Sunday."

As if his presence—it seemed now that he was alone—back here at Beechwood at this hour was expressly to deliver news meant for her. As if he had come with the unexpected information that she had no mother.

"There has been an accident, Jane. A fatal accident. Involving Paul Sheringham. Mister Paul at Upleigh."

She had the presence of mind, or mere mumbling reflex, to say, "At Upleigh?"

"No, Jane, not at Upleigh. A road accident. A car accident."

That was when he said, "You have gone very pale, Jane." It even seemed that he was stepping forward, arms held out, a little hesitantly but gallantly, because he thought she might be going to faint.

SHE WOULD NEVER know how Mr. Niven might have recorded his own version of this scene and all that followed. How he might have "written it," as it were. She would never know—but this was surely her own sudden panicky surmise—how much he *knew*.

She would never know (even at seventy or eighty) how much other people—people who weren't writers—did any of this stuff. It was a mystery.

Paul Sheringham didn't. She would have said she was sure of that. And that was—had been—his glory.

He had driven off (as she knew) when, unless some sorcery, some suspension of the laws of physics occurred, he would have been late. She knew (though she would never tell anyone) that he had made no effort to hurry—the opposite—though he was going to meet his bride-to-be. But he had made every effort, nonetheless, to prepare himself immaculately. This too only she would ever truly know, since after the impact the car had caught fire and his body was not only mangled but burnt. But items survived, she would learn, to suggest his state of attire—and his identity. An initialled cigarette case, a signet ring. The car itself was not so destroyed that it could not be readily identified as the car Paul Sheringham (often with some verve) drove.

But he would anyway have been significantly late. So that Emma Hobday's at first trivial but then intensifying feelings of bafflement, anger and indignation might have turned eventually into appalling conjecture. Good God—she had simply been stood up! Her husband-to-be had chosen this day—this marvellous day—to isolate her while he made his getaway. Law studies indeed! He had seized the opportunity of the house being completely deserted to—desert her! To drive off into the blue yonder. Because he could not face—it was only two weeks— marrying his betrothed wife. Or any other of his looming obligations. And this was his monstrous way of announcing it.

In short, she was being royally jilted. And, while she knew that her outraged imagination might just be getting the better of her and she could be becoming hysterical, some part of her—which knew Paul Sheringham—yet thought: And it might be just like him.

And so . . .

But only she, perhaps, Jane Fairchild, the maid at Beechwood, would "write" this scene. Emma Hobday wasn't a character in a book, was she? She hadn't invented her. She would never know how Emma Hobday herself might have written it.

And so . . . And so Miss Hobday couldn't just sit there, looking at her dainty wristwatch, could she, and being looked at by others? Her stomach unpleasantly rumbling. She had asked to use the hotel's telephone. This was all so unthinkable and embarrassing. But she was now at the centre of a world that was betraying her, undoing her appointed future. She had called first Upleigh House. No answer. The ringing telephone even seemed to be saying: This house is empty, there is no one here, no one listening. So then!

And then, after pacing this way and that and biting her lip, even going outside to draw deep breaths and look in all directions, and struggling with the thought that she really was behaving insanely, she had called the police. Perhaps the police might actually chase—chase and capture—her escaping fiancé, or come up with some other explanation that might at least save her from total ignominy.

And so, by that time of day, with information they by then would have had, the police would have had no alternative but to answer her enquiry and, yes, at least to save her from ignominy.

And so a further rapid and terrible succession of telephone calls had followed. The Swan at Bollingford was now ministering to a shocked woman who yet could still impart some vital details. Yes, the George Hotel at Henley. Further down the river. That's where they'd all gone, that's where they'd all be.

If they hadn't actually decided on some picnic. Or if they weren't, even now, on a sudden whim, cruising gaily and unreachably along the Thames on a hired launch. It had all been going to be like a sunny saluting of the imminent marriage—from which the happy couple themselves had judiciously excused themselves. If only they had meekly signed up to it.

But fortunately they were all still at the George, even still at their lunch table, still toying with sherry trifles.

And so everyone's day had changed utterly.

And so Mr. Niven had driven back here on his own, for reasons he was yet fully to explain. Though those can't have been—she might still have been anywhere, even by the banks of the Thames herself, enjoying her motherless Mothering Sunday—to announce it all to her.

"Jane, would you like to sit down?"

The only place would have been inside the Humber. Like Ethel and Iris. But she wasn't going to faint. She was still clutching the handlebars of her bicycle.

ALL THE AVAILABLE EVIDENCE was that—whatever had detained him—he was trying to minimise his lateness. He must have been driving fast at any rate. And he had taken the minor road which, though narrower and twistier, was a short cut, crossing the railway line by a bridge and so avoiding the level-crossing on the main road, which it might have been just his luck to find shut against him.

But he never crossed the railway line.

He was known to be a sometimes speedy yet

knowledgeable user of the local lanes. So he would certainly have known about the short cut—if you were heading for Bollingford—and known about the distinct right-hand bend the road made half a mile or so before the railway bridge. It was more of a corner in fact, indicating perhaps where surveyors and landowners had once failed to agree. There was even a large oak on the apex of the bend, marking the hazard. And Paul Sheringham had driven straight into it.

It was bright sunshine, a glorious day. There was no possibility that he had not *seen* the bend, the approaching, still leafless oak. There were road signs anyway. And he must have taken this bend scores of times. Perhaps his brakes had failed. The condition of the car could never reveal this. Perhaps—since no other traffic was involved—some innocent yet fatal factor, such as a stray farm animal, was responsible. Though would you crash into a tree to avoid a lesser, if significant, mishap?

The conclusion, even the formal verdict of an inquest, would be that a terrible—a "tragic"—accident had occurred. And this conclusion was reached not just from lack of witnesses or evidence to the contrary, but because it was the conclusion that everyone—the Sheringhams and Hobdays particularly, who had considerable connections with local officialdom—wished to reach. No one wished to believe that, two weeks before his marriage to Miss Emma Hobday and while actually driving to meet her, Paul Sheringham had driven fatally into a tree for any other reason than that it was an accident.

Mr. Sheringham senior would no doubt have explained, when asked, that because of the peculiarity of the day there would have been no one at Upleigh when his son departed. Both the cook and the maid, he would have stated, would have been at their mothers' homes. And this might have produced another breast-shaking spasm from Mrs. Sheringham. And the visiting policeman might have thought that he had asked questions enough, and put away his notebook.

But she, Jane Fairchild, would not have to answer any questions. Why should she? She was only the maid at Beechwood, not even at Upleigh. She had simply ridden off on her bicycle, and gone nowhere near, as it happened, the scene of the accident (though Mr. Niven might have thought that was why she had gone pale). Then she had returned, somewhat early.

And she had never heard—it was a never-spoken fact—as she wandered naked round that house any distant "crump." Would there have been a detectable "crump"? And she had never seen, in so far as she'd looked from any window, any smudge in that blue sky.

Though she had heard the telephone ring.

MR. NIVEN DIDN'T actually take hold of her. Not then. And she didn't faint, even if she had gone pale.

He repeated, "I'm so sorry, Jane, I'm so sorry to have to tell you this."

Why did it seem, at that complexion-changing moment, that she might have been someone else? It was an expression: "not to be yourself." Why did it seem that she might have been

Emma Hobday? Or that she might have been Mr. Niven's own daughter (though Mr. Niven didn't have one), who was also Emma Hobday. That Mr. Niven was, himself, Mr. Hobday. That the characters in this story had all been jumbled up.

Why did it seem that Mr. Niven was projecting onto her a whole confusion of scenes that she might have been in, but wasn't? She was only the maid—and, temporarily, not even that. Why did it seem that this day and its now terrible meaning—it wasn't Mothering Sunday any more at all—had blurred the usual order of things between herself and Mr. Niven?

He might have been speaking to his wife.

"Jane. Jane, I have left Clarissa—Mrs. Niven—with the others. In Henley. She felt she might be of better—service—there. Of course Emma—Miss Hobday—will drive to be with them. If she is able to. There was the question of whether they might all drive to her—to Bollingford. She is in Bollingford. Did I explain that? Or whether they might all drive to be at the Hobdays'. There is the question, Jane, of where everyone—ought to be. But I thought I should be here, Jane. I thought I should be here to . . ."

"Yes, Mr. Niven?"

"To go to Upleigh."

"Upleigh?"

"Yes. I stopped here first to use the telephone. I have just done so. I was just leaving. I have spoken to Clar—to Mrs. Niven. They are still at Henley. But they have decided to meet Miss Hobday—at the Hobdays'. That is the decision. I think that is the best plan. Miss Hobday must come first. Mr. and Mrs. Sheringham do not wish to return yet to Upleigh. Not yet. You can understand. I shall drive to the Hobdays' myself later. I am glad—I mean I am sorry—to be able to explain all this to you. But, Jane, you are back early—?"

"I thought, sir—it doesn't matter now—I might just come back here and read my book for a bit."

"Your book?"

"Yes."

"Well, if you— I mustn't—"

"It doesn't matter, Mr. Niven. My book doesn't matter."

"Someone must inform the staff at Upleigh, you see. Mr. Sheringham has told me that your—opposite number—is called Ethel. And the cook is called Iris."

"But—"

"Yes, I know, they have gone to their families. Like Milly. But they must be made aware as soon as possible of the—circumstances. Mr. and Mrs. Sheringham told me—oh good God—that Paul drove them both to the station this morning, but they will return separately. This—Ethel—most likely first. So I must go to Upleigh, you see, to await her. To inform her."

"Not the station, sir?"

Had she gone pale twice?

"That might not be the best place for such a purpose. In any case—how can I put this, Jane?"

"Put what, sir?"

"I feel that someone must—ascertain the situation at Upleigh in any case. I mean the situation as Mister Paul would have left it."

"But—"

"Yes, of course, he would simply have left the house. Good God, he was going to be brushing up on his law apparently. Yes, he would simply have left the house. There is no situation. But I feel—someone should check the situation. To prepare the Sheringhams. I mean, to reassure them. They are not ready to return there yet. They feel they should be with Miss Hobday. But you can imagine, Jane, you can imagine. The state of their— I offered to do what I have just told you. To make sure of things at Upleigh. They said that when he—when Mister Paul—left, and as the house would have been empty, he would have left a key, under a piece of stone—a stone pineapple, they said. Mrs. Sheringham said it was a stone pineapple. By the front porch. So—"

"So—?"

"I must drive to Upleigh. To wait for this Ethel. And to ascertain—"

Mr. Niven did not seem entirely ready for the task he had plainly volunteered for. He cleared his troubled throat.

"Jane—may I ask you something?"

"Ask me what, Mr. Niven?"

She was still gripping the handlebars of the

bicycle. She realised she was even squeezing its brake levers, though she was standing, quite still, beside it.

"If you would accompany me."

"Go with you, sir?"

"Of course, I understand it is still *your* day. If you wish, Jane, if you wish just to read your book—"

"*Your* book, Mr. Niven." She had no idea why she corrected him.

"Of course."

A brief contortion crossed his face, as if the beginning of a smile had turned into something else.

Was he going to sob? This wasn't his son. He was only an entangled neighbour.

"Yes, sir. I will go with you."

"I appreciate that, Jane. That is very good of you. I don't suppose you have ever been inside Upleigh House—"

"Would you mind, Mr. Niven, if I went in first and had a glass of water?"

"Yes—of course. Forgive me. This is all such a shock. And you have been cycling around all day! Yes, yes, of course, you will need to collect yourself, refresh yourself. Forgive me. I will be here, Jane, by the car, when you are ready."

AND PERHAPS that five minutes or so made all the difference. And when had it ever happened before: Mr. Niven waiting for *her*? Even standing by the car, when she reappeared, with its leather-lined door opened for her. She thought again of Ethel and Iris.

Inside the house—inside another empty house—her face had momentarily flooded, before she drenched it anyway with cold water. She might even have stifled a scream.

They drove to Upleigh. It was not a long drive at all. But he drove very slowly and carefully, as if to some appointment he might have wished not to be keeping. They found it hard to speak. Yes, she felt like Ethel. She might have been Ethel.

And as it happened, Ethel was ahead of them. The docile and dutiful Ethel had decided, as if unequipped for her day of freedom, to return in time even to make the Sheringhams their tea, should they themselves be back early enough to require it. Her "day" with her mother must have been a matter of just a couple of hours, and perhaps, for her own reasons, she had preferred not to stretch it out any longer. She would have alighted from the 3:42, then simply walked. It was only a mile or so. There were shortcuts through fields. The sun would have been turning a deeper gold. Primroses peeping, rabbits hopping. It would have taken the agile Ethel maybe twenty minutes. And they might have been the best twenty minutes of her day.

Even as they drove up the Upleigh drive, between the limes, she had seen the tell-tale sign: the upstairs window. Tell-tale only to her. It was closed now. Someone had closed it. Who else but Ethel? Ethel had been in the bedroom and closed the window.

And so she'd gasped—audibly to Mr. Niven—as they still drove up the drive. And Mr. Niven had taken it perhaps as a general gasp of distress, since they were both no doubt thinking—if in different ways—of how Paul Sheringham had driven down this very drive only hours ago in the opposite direction. For the last time. So Mr. Niven had said needlessly, "Yes, it's terrible, Jane."

And it *was* a gasp of distress, but it contained a small gasp of relief. And she otherwise betrayed nothing.

The sun was now off the front of the house and the gravel. When they got out of the car there was even a distinct chill in the air after the earlier heat of midday. And while Mr. Niven began looking for "this pineapple thing" and while she restrained herself from pointing at it or saying anything, Ethel suddenly opened the door—as she naturally would, since it seemed that there were visitors. She might even have thought, hearing the car from within, that it was Mr. and Mrs. Sheringham returning. But there she was on the porch suddenly, with a surprising air of being in charge of—of guarding—the whole edifice of Upleigh.

And as she watched Ethel open the door she naturally thought of when she had last seen it being opened.

"MR. NIVEN——?" Ethel had mustered, with a mixture of surprise and composure which didn't begin to embrace the puzzle of why Mr. Niven was there with Jane What-was-her-name, the maid from Beechwood.

Were all maids being offered rides today?

And Mr. Niven said, "You are Ethel, aren't you?" Which was also puzzling.

So there had been no need to wait for Ethel. She struggled, later, to imagine what that might have been like. And the whole procedure of informing Ethel took place at the front porch. Since Ethel plainly wouldn't be told to go in and sit down, not by Mr. Niven who wasn't her own master, even though it was clear from his manner that something really awful might be about to be uttered. And was that Beechwood girl supposed to be coming inside and sitting down too?

Ethel, in fact, suddenly changed. Or perhaps her true Ethelness appeared. She would never know if her (and even Paul Sheringham's) whole conception of Ethel had been mistaken from the beginning.

Ethel's eyes, even as Mr. Niven was grappling with words again, had suddenly bored into her own as if she, Ethel Bligh, knew everything. Though equally they might have been saying, just as unswervingly, "We maidservants have to stick together, don't we, and know our place in the world?"

Her look went a lot further anyway than a mere bewildered, "And what are *you* doing here? What are you doing consorting with your master?"

Behind Ethel, she could just make out, through the vestibule and the shadows of the hall, the table and the bowl with the white clusters of orchids. It was somehow incredible that they should still be there.

"I have some distressing news, Ethel," Mr. Niven began. "If I may call you Ethel?"

"Yes, sir."

And so Ethel was informed. And stood there, like an unbudging defender on the front porch, as if she were fully prepared, now so much harm had apparently come to this house, to prevent any further assaults upon it. Mr. Niven, who was still on the gravel below, seemed to cower before her sudden authority.

"Then it is just as well, Mr. Niven, I came back early, so I can be of assistance. I must have known in my bones something was wrong. That I might be needed. Mr. and Mrs. Sheringham—they must be quite beside themselves. They must be in such a state, again." Ethel had said that deliberate "again." "I will be here for them when they return. I will inform Cook when she returns. I will take—I will make, if required any telephone calls."

"Ethel—"

But Ethel had carried on, perhaps in rare defiance, for her, of the speak-when-spoken-to rule.

"I have already tidied around. I have tidied Mister Paul's room—"

"That is just the point, Ethel."

"The point, Mr. Niven?"

"I need to ask you— I am here to ascertain—" Mr. Niven floundered. "Did you find anything, in Mister Paul's room?"

"Anything? I don't know what you mean, Mr. Niven."

"Like—a note, Ethel. Anything written."

"No, sir. I did not find anything written. And I would not have read it if I had, sir." Ethel almost looked as if her next words might have been a snappy, "Would that be all, sir?" Or even a "And what business would that be of yours?"

"Then— That is all right, Ethel. That is all—all right."

"Are *you* all right, sir? Would you be requiring a cup of tea or anything?"

"No, thank you, Ethel. Are *you* all right? Would you require—our company? Or Jane here's company?"

That was a possibility she, the Beechwood maid, hadn't been prepared for and she waited, surrenderingly, for Ethel's grasping of the initiative.

"No, sir. I can manage, thank you."

But she had said it not looking at Mr. Niven, but squarely, unwaveringly at her "opposite number."

And her look was like the look of the sternest and most forgiving of parents.

SO, SHE WOULD NEVER know many things. But she knew now that, certainly by the time the Sheringhams returned, Ethel would have thoroughly "tidied up" Mister Paul's room. The flung-aside trousers, the bedclothes. The sheets would have been replaced (though no one, Ethel must later have reflected on this, was going to sleep in them), the removed ones bundled into the laundry basket, waiting for Monday's copper. The kitchen table—a simple kindness to Cook Iris—would have been cleared and cleaned And everything returned to as it should be. Even though everything was different.

And Ethel would one day find her way into another minor (not so minor) character—in *If the Truth Be Known*. She would be transmuted and (though only the author would know) honoured by fiction. She would not be called Ethel (she would be called Edith) or be anything like Ethel, or even be a maid, but she would be one of those characters who exist, seemingly, on the periphery of things and yet know everything. And she would be one of those characters whose real "character" goes for most of the time unsuspected and unperceived. But that was a general truth she, the author, would know by then to apply to the creation of character in fiction, as it was a general truth about life and people.

But she would never know exactly how much Ethel had known all along. And she would never know what Ethel did or thought or imagined or felt when she was left alone again in that house in the interval before the Sheringhams (and Cook Iris) returned, and even, in time, the police appeared, just for some routine questions.

She would hardly have composed a thank-you note to her mother.

THEY DROVE BACK. The sun was dipping and turning orange. The afternoon was waning. And crispening. It was only March. Ethel would light fires too, no doubt, among her other tasks. The right thing to do in the circumstances, keep the home fires burning. Just as she herself would do soon, when she became a maid again at Beechwood.

What was she now, for the time being?

Mr. Niven said, after a long silence, "I'm sorry to have kept you from your reading, Jane. I'm so sorry to have used up your time. What is the book at present? I forget."

"It's all right, sir. It doesn't matter."

She was sitting beside him in the front seat, where, when her husband drove, Mrs. Niven would sit. She was trying very hard not to weep, to hold herself together.

If only Mr. Niven might say, "You must take the evening off. You must take a long hot bath." But maids never took long hot baths or were given unscheduled evenings off, especially when they had had the day off anyway. In a little while she would have to resume her duties. She would have to be at least as strong as Ethel.

The gathering evening, the apricot light, the gauzy green-gold world, was impossibly beautiful.

After another long silence he said, "That's all five of them, Jane."

She knew what he meant. She knew exactly what he meant. But she said, "Yes, sir," in the way that maids simply mouth those words in general concurrence with everything.

Then, when they'd turned into the sweep in front of Beechwood and he'd switched off the engine he suddenly leant across to her and, like a child, wept—blubbed—even pressed his head, his face to her breasts, so that she thought of when she'd pressed them—had it been only this afternoon?—to the opened pages of a book. "I'm so sorry, Jane, I'm so sorry," he said, even as his face remained where it was. And she said, involuntarily cradling the back of his head, "That's quite all right, Mr. Niven, that's quite all right."

THE BOOK WAS called *Youth*—the book she might have read on the bench in the garden, or might have mentioned to Mr. Niven when he'd asked. She might have just uttered the odd word "youth."

Or rather it was called *Youth, a Narrative; and Two Other Stories*, a clumsy, unexciting mishmash of a title. It was the only book by Joseph Conrad in the Beechwood library, and the narrative called *Youth* was the first thing in it and a good place anyway to start, since, as she would come to know, it was loosely based on Conrad's own early experiences and on his first encounter (she would come to know that he wrote about it often) with a thing—a vision, a promise, a fact, an illusion—called "the East."

It was anyway what, on that Mothering Sunday, she'd only just begun, and if her day had gone differently, if the telephone hadn't rung, she might quite easily have finished it in some sunny corner of Berkshire or even in the Beechwood garden. She might even have got on to the *Other Stories*. One of them was called "Heart of Darkness" and as it turned out (her Mothering Sunday having turned out as it did) it was a long time before she got round to that story, even though she knew she had discovered in Joseph Conrad someone important. It was the forbidding title perhaps.

She knew that Conrad was different from anything else she had read, but she could sense that there were things she might not be ready for. It was a little like reading *Treasure Island* and *Kidnapped* but not wanting yet to read *Dr. Jekyll and Mr. Hyde*.

She quite liked the word "narrative," it was a sober, dependable-sounding word, but she didn't see why the one thing should be called a narrative and the other things just stories. The word she most liked in those days was "tale"—and she was glad to find out that Conrad often preferred it too. There was something more enticing about calling something a tale rather than a story, but this had to do, perhaps, with the suggestion that it might not be wholly truthful, it might have a larger element of invention.

About all these words—"tale," "story," even "narrative"—there was a sort of question, always hovering in the background, of truth, and it might be hard to say how much truth went with each. There was also the word "fiction"— one day this would be the very thing she dealt in—which could seem almost totally dismissive of truth. A complete fiction! Yet something that was clearly and completely fiction could also contain—this was the nub and the mystery of the matter—truth. When she had read all three of them, she felt she could say *Dr. Jekyll and Mr. Hyde* was more truthful than *Treasure Island* or *Kidnapped*. Though some people might say it was the weirdest and certainly the most frightening of the lot.

"Telling tales": it could have the sense of concocting downright lies. Like "spinning yarns." It seemed in fact that "yarn" might be the best word for those adventure books she'd been first drawn to in the library at Beechwood, and to have questioned whether those books were truthful would have been pointless. They were yarns. In the word "yarn" itself there was a salty tang of men and the sea. And so many of those "boys' books" she read had involved, one way or another, going to sea—a voyage, an unknown land—as if that was the essence of adventure and what every boy wanted to do. And here was Joseph Conrad who seemed to have been just one of those boys.

And she liked the word "youth." Or rather she was challenged by it, because it wasn't in any obvious way like the title of a tale, story or narrative—or adventure. It seemed more like just an idea. Yet when she had first flipped through the pages of *Youth* in the Beechwood library it had seemed to be full of all that seafaring, yarny stuff she was already familiar with. Perhaps it was what one of the Niven boys, or by then young men, had thought too, though it was obvious he hadn't got very far with the book, if he'd read it at all. Unlike other books in the revolving bookcase, it still looked clean and new. It even bore an inscription, in dark-blue ink,

"J. Niven, Oct. 1915," that looked fresh enough to have been written yesterday. And maybe that was another reason why she picked it out.

Conrad, she soon felt, might be generally called a "challenging author." "Heart of Darkness" . . . Maybe J. Niven had thought this too. "Challenging author" was not yet part of her writer-judging vocabulary and certainly not a phrase she could imagine one day being applied to herself. She would take it, when it was, as a complimentary phrase, but of course there were people who used it adversely. It was another way of saying "off-putting." Well, that was their bloody problem.

"CONRAD," she would say, when answering another of those repeated and bothersome questions. "Oh Conrad—he was the one." As if she were talking about someone she had met. Which in a sense she had.

"Oh Conrad, I used to love all that seafaring stuff."

"But a man's author, don't you think?"

"And your point is . . . ?"

The other reason why she liked the word "youth" was of course that it was what she had—then. She was "a youth." Although there was a way in which "youth," like "yarn," had a strongly masculine bias to it. A man could be a "youth," but a woman? But then everything had a masculine bias in 1924.

There was in any case a question—and the word "youth" seemed to have a rubbery quality to it to accommodate this—about where youth began and where it turned into something else. But, surely, still at twenty-two. In 1924 even the century was still in its youth ... Though, in fact, that wasn't the case at all. Youth—great swathes of it—was just what the century had lost.

And, yes, of course, by 1924 Conrad was arguably outmoded, already behind the times. Sailing ships? The exotic East? Didn't he know what had happened to the world?

BUT HE WAS truly the one. On the night of Mothering Sunday 1924, when, for good reasons, she was utterly unable to sleep or rest, she picked up again Joseph Conrad's *Youth*. What else could she do? Cry? And cry again? In her little plank of a bed. People read books, didn't they, to get away from themselves, to escape the troubles of their lives?

And it was and it wasn't an adventure story. It was different, it had something special. It was about five crusty old men sitting round a table—yarning—who had done different things with their lives, but had all once been at sea, in their youth. She could see the men at the table, see their lined faces. One of them was called Marlow and it was he who told his story. It wasn't really an adventure story at all. It was about a dumpy old ship that was always having bad luck, never getting far from murky home waters, but which one day, at the end of the story, which was also a sort of beginning, finally makes it to—the East.

WHEN SHE HAD finished *Youth and Other Stories*, even managing to read "Heart of Darkness"— which was indeed challenging and truly like nothing else she had read—she knew she had to get more Conrad, and so she'd written to a bookshop in Reading which sent books by post. She had the half-crown still that Mr. Niven had given her, not to mention other half-crowns put by. She could buy a postal order in the village. And dealing with a bookshop in this enterprising way perhaps even made her think: A bookshop, a bookshop . . .

She bought a book called *Lord Jim*, which was not unlike *Youth*, but much longer—and challenging. It was called a "tale." It involved that man Marlow again, and it was tempting to think that Marlow was really Conrad in disguise. Then she bought a book called *The Secret Agent*, which was quite different, since it wasn't set in the East or to do with ships, but set in the grubby streets of London, though it still had that feeling of entering unknown and possibly dangerous territory which, if she'd had the word, she might have called "Conradian."

By then she'd think that Conrad himself must be a sort of secret agent, slipping between worlds. And much later she'd think and sometimes say that all writers are secret agents. But perhaps the truth was—though she wouldn't say this—that we are all secret agents, that's what we are.

Anyway, by the time she'd read *The Secret Agent*, and foolish as it might have been, she had formed her own secret wish to become a writer. And she was not unused to having secrets.

It wasn't his real name—Conrad—she found out, since he was really Polish. So he had a name a little like hers. It wasn't a pen name either, it was just his "English" name. But the remarkable, the truly astonishing thing about Joseph Conrad was that in order to write all his books, he hadn't just had to learn how to write, but to write in a *whole new language*. That was almost unbelievable. It was like crossing some impossible— impassable—barrier, and she felt that perhaps that was the greater thing, the greater achievement and truer adventure, greater even than going on all those voyages in his youth, more thrilling even than reaching the East.

And it was what she would have to do to become a writer: cross an impossible barrier. And she too, she would come to understand this, would have to find a language, even though she

had a language, since finding a language, finding *the* language—that was what, she would
come to understand, writing really was. But she
would seldom say these things in interviews
either. They were too near the bone.

"Conrad, oh yes—he had something special."
As if she might have been talking about some
old lover.

And, if the truth be known, in her last months
at Beechwood and before she "went to Oxford"
it became a thrill for her to know that Joseph
Conrad, who'd been born in Poland and had
sailed the seas, was actually alive then, somewhere not so far away, in the folds of England. A
thrill that couldn't last long, though she'd been
alive to know it, because one morning in August
1924—it was like a sudden personal shock—
she'd read in the paper, before reflattening it and
putting it on Mr. Niven's breakfast table, that
Joseph Conrad had died.

And, if the truth be known (though she would
never say this, in interviews or to anyone), all
the pictures she'd got to see of Joseph Conrad—
the later Conrad—had made her fall in love

with him. The gravity, the beard, the expression in his eyes as if he were seeing something far off that was also deep inside. She had even sometimes imagined what it might be like to lie in bed with Conrad, just to lie beside him, not speaking, a naked, ageing Conrad, both of them looking up and watching the smoke from their cigarettes rising, mingling under the ceiling, as if the smoke held some truth greater than either of them could find words for.

The first sigh of the East on my face. That I can never forget.

SHE WOULD BECOME a writer. She would write books. She would write nineteen novels. She would even become a "modern writer." Though how long do you remain "modern"? It was like the word "youth." And was that what writing was about anyway: modernity? She would know times and changes, and write about them. She would live to be over ninety, nearly a hundred, and in her later years when she developed a definite mischievous streak and when she was wheeled out yet again—"Jane Fairchild at Eighty," "Jane Fairchild at Ninety"—she would mention the names of writers of the past as if, once upon a time, they had actually been her friends

All the scenes. All the real ones and all the ones in books. And all the ones that were somehow in-between, because they were only what you could picture and imagine of real people. Like trying to picture her mother. Or only what you could suppose might have been true, if things had turned out differently, once, long ago. She might have gone with him, it might somehow have been magically arranged, to stand, pressed close to him, by the rail, in the chill of the dawn, as the sun unfurled great fiery carpets across the downs and as Fandango drew close, nostrils flaring and steaming, hooves pounding. She might have understood it and known it for ever. The fourth leg? The fourth leg was hers.

She would tell in her books many stories. She would even begin to tell, in her later careless years, stories about her own life, in such a way that you could never quite know if they were true or made up. But there was one story she would never tell. On some things she would be as impeccably silent as Ethel (who became Edith after all) proved to be. As silent as, she supposed, Joseph Conrad, for all his story-telling genius, would have been about some things, lying there beside her like some wonderful hollow husk of a man.

Telling stories, telling tales. Always the implication that you were trading in lies. But for her it would always be the task of getting to the quick, the heart, the nub, the pith: the trade of truth-telling. It had been Donald's task too, in his way. Poor Donald, taken away from her forty, fifty years ago.

Enough of this interview claptrap and chicanery. So what was it then exactly, this truth-telling? They would always want even the explanation explained! And any writer worth her salt would lead them on, tease them, lead them up the garden path. Wasn't it bloody obvious? It was about being true to the very stuff of life, it was about trying to capture, though you never could, the very feel of being alive. It was about finding a language. And it was about being true to the fact, the one thing only followed from the other, that many things in life—oh so many more than we think—can never be explained at all.

A NOTE ON THE TYPE

This book was set in a typeface called Walbaum. The original cutting of this face was made by Justus Erich Walbaum (1768–1839) in Weimar in 1810. The type was revived by the Monotype Corporation in 1934. Although this type may be classified as modern, numerous slight irregularities in its cut give it its humane manner.

Composed by North Market Street Graphics, Lancaster, Pennsylvania

Printed and bound by RR Donnelley, Crawfordsville, Indiana

Designed by Cassandra J. Pappas

How I Survived My Summer Vacation

Darcy & Duanne Jahns

Cover by
Doug Martin

Scholastic Canada Limited

Scholastic Canada Ltd.
123 Newkirk Road, Richmond Hill, Ontario, Canada L4C 3G5

Scholastic Inc.
555 Broadway, New York, NY 10012, USA

Ashton Scholastic Limited
Private Bag 92801, Penrose, Auckland, New Zealand

Ashton Scholastic Pty Limited
PO Box 579, Gosford, NSW 2250, Australia

Scholastic Publications Ltd.
Villiers House, Clarendon Avenue, Leamington Spa,
Warwickshire CV32 5PR, UK

Canadian Cataloguing In Publication Data

Jahns, Duanne
  How I survived my summer vacation

ISBN 0-590-74043-1

I. Jahns, Darcy. II. Title.

PS8569.A45H6 1991   jC813'.54   C91-094301-X
PZ7.J34Ho 1991

6 5 4 3 2   Printed in Canada   4 5 6 7 / 9
                 Manufactured by Gagné Printing

For Mom and Mena

— Duanne and Darcy

Contents

1

Memories of a Survivor

"Frieda, I know you're down there staring at your report card. Now put it away and come set the table! It's just about supper time."

That was my mom. She hates tardiness at meals, snakes anywhere near her face, my grandma's dinosaur thighs (she says she inherited them), and Def Leppard. She's basically a nice person.

"What are we having? Oh, gross — elephant boogies!"

That was my brother Stanley. He's thirteen and really wormy-looking. He hates me, my sister Margot, and oysters (I think that's what we're having for supper). He's also stupid.

"Margot, you've been on that phone so long the cord's hot! Now tell whoever it is to call back later and come help your mother. It's supper time!"

That was my dad. He hates phone calls during meals, the neighbour's dog (it doo-doos on our lawn every day), and my sister's hair (it's green).

"Geez, Dad, get a heart! Can't a person have any privacy around here? No, Mark, I gotta go. My dad's having a hyperspasm again. Yeah. I'll call you back when they're not listening."

That was Margot. She hates being related to us, being fourteen, and all of Dad's clothes. She wants to be a dancer on *The Party Machine*.

And then there's me, Frieda Farkas. I had just passed grade five, and I still hadn't figured out why.

Ignoring all the turmoil upstairs, I looked at my final report card for the hundredth time since Mrs. Crowell, my home room teacher, had given it to me that afternoon. It was pretty crumpled and smeary looking — I guess from being constantly opened, closed, clutched to my heart with relief, then opened again.

At first I had thought it was a mistake. I couldn't possibly have passed, not after the crummy year I had. You see, I'm not exactly an all-star student. I do pretty poorly in most subjects except arithmetic. That one I fail.

It had to be a typing error. I even imagined how it could have happened. I saw Mr. Collins, the gym teacher, coming into the principal's office and making another pass at Miss Baxter, the secretary. I saw her get so flustered she accidentally checked off the *Passed* box instead of the *Failed* when she was typing up my report card.

But I quickly realized that couldn't possibly be what happened. Miss Baxter is a deadly typist, and not in the least the flustery type. Why, once she found a mouse in the drawer of her desk, and several grade six kids swore they saw her squash it with her dictionary. Eeww, that must have been really gross! They said the book had to be burned.

So if Mr. Collins wasn't responsible for the mistake, there had to be some other explanation. My best friend Marcy Mae Peterson told me to just forget it — my report card was correct, I really did pass.

"How can you be so sure?" I demanded as we walked home together after school like we always did. Ahead, Billy Rosetta and his friend Shaun Towers were shooting navy beans at us through milk shake straws. They were such lousy shots, the beans were whizzing way over our heads. "I'll bet you anything Mrs. Crowell is going to come chasing after me any minute now and tell me she gave me the wrong report card."

"Oh, don't be so silly, Frieda," said Marcy with

a quick toss of her curly red head. "You passed. You really did!"

"I don't know," I said, looking anxiously over my shoulder. I thought I could hear heavy footsteps approaching, but it was just some fat kid crossing the street. "I don't think I did. Nothing good ever happens to me, not without a catch. I think I'm cursed."

Marcy groaned, exasperated. "Will you stop being such a pessimist? You didn't fail! Jeepers, if I didn't know any better I'd think you wanted to fail!"

"No, I don't want to," I assured her. "I just expected to."

Marcy knew what I was talking about. Grade five hadn't been my best year. In fact, I can't remember a year that went as badly. It all started in September when I bombed on a dumb arithmetic test and got stuck in the special ed. class with Kenny Marks. Do you know what it's like to sit beside a person who eats peanut butter and onion sandwiches for breakfast? Mrs. Crowell kept a geranium on our table. It died.

Then I cheated on a social studies test with Iva Jean Conners. What a stupid thing to do! Iva Jean couldn't get the last two questions on the test, so I let her see my paper. But Mrs. Crowell caught us, and boy, was she angry! I thought her head was going to split open and flames shoot out of her eyes. Iva Jean and I were so scared! She gave us both a big fat zero on the test, and then she called our parents. That's when we were really punished. I got grounded for a month.

Then, as if that wasn't bad enough, the really terrible thing happened — my science project got loose in the school! To this day I don't know how it happened. I was sure I closed the lid on the old fish tank I was keeping my garter snake in, but I guess I didn't. When I told Mrs. Crowell what had happened she just rolled her eyes up at the ceiling and muttered, "Frieda Farkas, why doesn't this surprise me?" Then she sent all of us grade five kids home, called in the pest control people, and had the classroom fogged.

No doubt about it. When you consider all the things that happened to me, my year was pretty crummy.

"Cheer up, Frieda," said Marcy, easily dodging an oncoming navy bean. "You're not cursed. You may think you are, but really you aren't. In fact, you're really very fortunate."

"Fortunate!" I stared at her with eyes so big they could have doubled as jar lids. "How do you figure that?"

"Well, don't you see? You made it! It's not all the bad things that happen to a person that count, it's how you get through them. And you made it, Frieda. You're a survivor! You got through grade five and survived! That's the important thing, don't you think?"

I scratched my head silently for a moment. My spiky brown hair was so stiff with mousse I almost cut my fingers. A survivor. I had never thought about it that way before. Hmm, maybe Marcy had a point. Maybe I *was* a survivor.

The idea stayed with me all afternoon. And slowly, the more I looked at my report card, the more I began to realize that Marcy must be right. I was a survivor. I did make it. Grade five might have been hard, but I had passed and that was the important thing.

I hugged my crumpled report card one last time and savoured the good feeling it gave me. I even moved some of the junk off my dresser so I could fit it under a clip on my mirror, right between my lucky dinosaur key chain and my to-die-for picture of River Phoenix. Just as I was stepping back to admire the effect I heard the basement door open again, and Mom yelled, "Frieda! If you don't come up here right now and set this table we're going to eat off the floor! Do you hear me?"

"Mom," wailed Margot in the background, "Stanley's looking at me again! Make him quit it!"

"Oh, my God!" shouted Dad. "That dog is on our lawn again! Someone call the police!"

I took one last glance at the mirror and turned off the light. I had made it through a whole year of school. But could I get through a whole summer vacation with my family?

"You're a survivor, Frieda," I kept telling myself as I slowly went upstairs. "Remember that — you're a survivor."

2

That Thing That Starts With a D

There are two things I can always count on every summer: one, we'll go camping, and two, everyone will get that thing that starts with a D. The last is because of the first, and the first is because of my dad. After all, it's always his dumb idea.

Now I love my dad, and he says he loves me too. But every year when he drives us out to the middle of nowhere and makes us spend two weeks living like Neanderthals I really start to wonder. I've asked Mom a thousand times what makes him think bathing out of a soup can is a vacation. In between her sobs she always says the same thing: "This is something we must do for your father. It's important to him."

"But, Mom," I remind her, "we always get . . . you know."

And she always bites her lip nervously, squeezes my hand, and whispers, "Be brave, Frieda. Be brave."

I didn't have to be a psychic to know this year wasn't going to be any different. The morning after school ended I walked into the kitchen and found Dad and Stanley hunched over a map with a magnifying glass. From their excited expressions I could tell they had just found either the site of Captain Kidd's treasure or the location of our upcoming summer vacation.

"Loretta, here it is!" exclaimed Dad. "We've found the perfect place to go camping. How does Skeleton Lake sound to you?"

"Like a hint," Mom replied, worried. She, Margot, and I bent over the map, and our eyes settled on Dad's finger. When we realized exactly where he was pointing they nearly popped out of our heads.

"Oh, Richard!" Mom gasped. "It's so far north!"

"Not really," Dad assured us. "It's only about five hours from here. Six hours tops."

"But it's so . . . isolated!"

"That's the beauty of it," he said solemnly. "We're going to be in God's country."

I swallowed hard and turned to Margot. "Does that mean we're going to die and go to heaven?" I whispered.

"We can only hope," she muttered back.

"Look, Richard," Mom kept trying, "just how do you plan to get us up there? I don't see any roads."

"Yeah," agreed Margot. "Like, I'm not going if we have to ride pack mules or anything."

I looked at the location again and thought maybe dog sleds would be more appropriate.

"Now everyone just relax," said Dad firmly. "I was talking to a guy at work who went up there last year, and he said there's a really good service road that'll take us right to the beach."

"But, Dad, why do we have to go camping again?" whined Margot. "I'm just starting to be able to go into a bathroom without checking it first for wildlife, and that's after a whole year. Why can't we do something else this summer?"

The room went silent. Then Dad's speech #146, *We Are Family, Hear Us Roar,* kicked in. He stood up and stared at the three of us. His eyes were glassy and his bottom lip trembled.

"It's because we are a family," he said slowly. "This is the only time of the year we can all be together, learning about life and nature the way it was meant to be — in the wilderness."

"I'm sure we could learn just as much from a hotel," countered Margot.

"Ah, yes, but can a hotel give us the thrill of

pulling in a fat rainbow trout? Can a hotel give us the peace of viewing a moose with her young feeding in a creek? Can a hotel give us the joy of sitting beside a crackling fire and counting the fireflies?"

I wiped at the tear sliding down my cheek and saw Mom doing the same. Like I said, I love my dad.

"Well, can it?" he asked again.

"No, I guess not," mumbled Margot. "I just thought we might be . . . safer . . . if we stayed in a hotel."

A wide grin stretched across Dad's face, and he slipped his arm around Stanley's thin shoulders. "There's no need to worry," he said confidently. "There are plenty of men around here to take care of you."

I looked at my brother and was still worried. He had a ruler in his mouth. He was either eating it or trying to measure his tongue.

"What do you say, everyone?" cheered on Dad. "Why don't we all get into the spirit of this?" He was stabbing the air with his finger for emphasis. "Let's all pitch in and get ready for fourteen days of fun and excitement!"

I've often thought that camping might not be so bad if we did it like normal people do, like Marcy and her family do — roughing it in a thirty-foot motor home. Instead we have to settle for moving most of our house into the car.

For the rest of that day we pushed, pulled and dragged the tent and everything we thought we'd need outside and stuffed it all into the station wagon. By the time we finished the only way Dad could drive was if Mom stuck her head out the side window and yelled directions. And if Margot and I wanted to go along — which neither of us did — we had to take turns sitting on each other's knees. I guess we could have sat on Stanley, but that would have meant actually touching him. By five o'clock the next morning we were on the road.

It took us seven hours to drive to Skeleton Lake, and that's not counting the hour we wasted at the last gas station. Margot thought she saw Elvis and made us all get out and look. During the trip there were sixty-eight "Drop dead, creep!"s, eighty-nine "You jerk!"s, forty-six "Stop touching me!"s, sixteen "Richard, why did we have children?"s, and seventy-one "Stop that bloody noise or I'll give you one!"s. The last time Dad really did stop the car and give us one. By early afternoon we had reached our destination and were standing on the beach.

"Just smell that air, will you!" said Dad excitedly as he filled his lungs with another deep breath.

"Isn't that something?"

"You're not kidding," muttered Mom. She pinched her nose to block off the stink coming from a couple of dead fish lying near her. "I wonder why the maintenance men haven't cleaned the beach."

Dad and Stanley looked at each other and burst out laughing.

"Maintenance men!" Dad snorted. "There are no maintenance men here. Why, there isn't another soul around for at least a hundred kilometres!"

"A hundred kilometres!" echoed Mom, sick.

"We're doomed," mumbled Margot.

"But, Richard, what if we run into trouble?" asked Mom. "What if we have an emergency?"

Stanley elbowed Margot. "Like what?" he sneered. "Like you chip a fingernail?"

"No, like I chip your head," she threatened.

"Now, now," said Dad, stepping between them. "There'll be no chipping of heads on this trip. It's all for one and one for all, remember? We're experienced campers, and if we watch out for each other we'll be safe."

Yeah, right, I thought.

When it comes to camping, Mom calls Dad a romantic fool. I think that's because whenever he shaves with a jackknife while staring at his reflection in a piece of tin foil, he thinks he looks like Daniel Boone. Margot says he looks more like Pat Boone, especially if he's wearing his black dress socks and sandals. I tend to agree. After all, would Daniel Boone let his family live on canned zucchini and Spork for three days in a row? I think not.

On the fourth day Mom got mad and dug out the fishing rods. She told Dad if he ever hoped to see her smile again, he'd go out and kill something. Unfortunately he decided to take Stanley with him.

Now I know my dad loves Stanley and Stanley loves him. But there have to be times when even Dad seriously wonders whether my brother did some permanent noggin damage a few years back when he was riding his bicycle with a paper bag on his head and crashed into the side of the garage. Let's face it, Stanley is a walking disaster area. Already in the first three days of this trip he had given the car a sunroof (he was chopping wood and the axe slipped out of his hands) and forced us all to spend a night sleeping under spruce trees (Mom told him to pitch the tent and he did — right into the lake). Now Dad wanted to go out with him on open water in a rubber dinghy! Scary.

While the two "men" paddled out to the middle of the lake, Mom, Margot, and I sat on the beach and took turns watching through a pair of binoculars. Surprisingly enough, everything seemed to go all right. That is, until Stanley picked up his fishing rod.

"Oooh, wow!" squealed Margot suddenly. "Like, when did we get a speedboat?"

Mom and I squinted at the two orange life preservers that were now little more than dots in the distance whizzing along the horizon.

"And how come Dad and Stanley are getting bigger?" continued Margot.

Mom took the binoculars away from my sister and looked for herself. "Oh, my God!" she gasped. "They're not getting bigger, the dinghy's getting smaller. They've sprung a leak!"

"Oooh, bummer," Margot and I breathed sympathetically.

Luckily the dinghy coasted toward the shore, and Dad and Stanley only had to swim a short way towing a deflated bag of rubber behind them. By the time they got out of the water Stanley must have apologized a hundred times and asked Dad if he was going to kill him a thousand.

"Stanley, will you stop apologizing," said Dad tiredly. "I'm not mad at you. It wasn't your fault; accidents happen. Now go and get the tire repair kit."

"Tire repair kit?" repeated Stanley blankly.

"Yeah, the kit I gave you to put in the glove compartment. We do have it, don't we?"

"Uh, not exactly."

"What do you mean?"

"I kinda left it in the cupboard at home."

"Stanley?"

"What?"

"Now I'm going to kill you."

Since we couldn't use the dinghy and all of our fishing equipment was on the bottom of the lake, Dad resorted to standing on the shore and dangling a safety pin on a string tied to a stick. To everyone's surprise, he caught three fish. That really boosted Dad's ego, not to mention how it impressed Mom. She started calling him "my big caveman," and for the rest of the day we had to listen to endless recitals of speech #61, *Necessity: The Mother of Invention.*

Unfortunately all through supper I kept thinking back to the first fish we had seen lying on the beach. I couldn't help wondering if the reason Dad's fish had been so close to shore was because they were looking for a place to die too. But of course I didn't say anything.

We didn't die from starvation this trip, but we almost expired from boredom. Dad tried hard to keep us occupied with educational things, but there's only so much of *Know Your Water Bugs and Slime* Margot and I can take. Actually I didn't know which was worse — going on another nature hike with Dad or staying at the campsite with nothing to do.

Then it started to rain. For two days all of us were stuck in the tent. Guessing the expiry dates on canned goods and devising ways to trap small game in Mom's hair rollers became our only forms of entertainment.

By the time the sun came back out we were all pretty testy. Who am I kidding? We were downright hostile. Mom and Dad were using phrases like legal separation, and Margot was threatening to run away — to home. Finally that night after supper we called a temporary cease-fire. We decided to sit around the campfire and watch the sun set together. It was really nice.

Just when it was getting dark a deep growling noise sounded from Dad's direction.

"Same to you, fella," said Mom.

"I never said anything," Dad defended himself. "It was my stomach. Boy, I don't feel too good."

"Maybe you should go and lie down," she suggested.

Dad left, but after the rest of us had sung

seventeen choruses of "Kum Ba Ya" he came back.
"Loretta," he announced, "I've got diarrhea."
Margot groaned. "Oh, gross! He's sleeping by the door tonight."
"What did he say?" I asked Mom hesitantly.
"That thing that starts with a D has arrived," she replied wearily. Then she said to Dad hopefully, "It's probably just a touch of stomach flu. You should be better in the morning."

Unfortunately he wasn't better the next morning. And by then he wasn't the only one with a problem. During the night it had hit the rest of us too. Mom decided it couldn't be the flu like she first thought. It could only be food poisoning, and the culprit must have been our supper — a wild root and mushroom stew Dad had slow-cooked all afternoon.

By noon, when no one was showing any signs of improvement, Mom declared defeat. "Richard," she announced, "we're going home."

"Hallelujah!" said Margot, and bolted for the car.

"But, Loretta, we can't go now," Dad pleaded. "We've got three more days of vacation left."

"Too bad. I think you've had enough camping for one year. I know I have. Besides, the squirrels just ate the last of our Pepto-Bismol tablets and we're down to one roll of toilet paper. Now pack the car."

We all held our breath, waiting for Dad's reply. When he finally spoke it almost killed him.

"Oh, all right," he mumbled. "Let's go."

I fairly danced with joy. Our vacation was over!

"Thank you, God," I rejoiced, supremely grateful we were leaving. For once I was even grateful for that thing that starts with a D.

3

A Soldier's Story

July 16
Dear Diary:
Today I declared war on Stanley. He has done the unthinkable. He told Jeremy Hurlbut that I love him. I'm so embarrassed! I HATE Jeremy Hurlbut. Jeremy Hurlbut is a pig who picks his nose and eats it — I've seen him! He lives on the same street as us with his horrid dog Timber. He catches birds and chases little kids. So does Timber. I wish they lived somewhere else, like Pluto. With Stanley. I'm not talking to my brother.

July 17
Dear Diary:
This is the last straw. Stanley told Jeremy that I want to go out with him and probably marry him

when I get older. I want to die! He also said if I don't do all his chores for two weeks he'll tell Margaret Crampton the same thing, and she'll tell all my friends, and they'll all laugh at me. Margaret would believe Stanley too. She hates me. She also has a big mouth. (Really. Once I saw her stuff two hot dogs and a handful of corn chips in it.) I'm doomed. I'll probably have to leave the country. Maybe I'll go to Peru. I hope it's far away.

July 18
Dear Diary:

This is getting out of control. Stanley has to be stopped. I don't want to do his chores, but I don't want him to spread lies about me either. I went to Mom today and told her what he was doing. But Stanley denied it, and Mom just told me I shouldn't falsely accuse people. It's true though. He's blackmailing me, and I'm all alone. I have to figure out a way to stop him. I don't know how yet, but I'll find a way. In the meantime, I'm doing all his chores just to keep him quiet. But I refuse to smile while I'm doing them.

July 19
Dear Diary:

My luck is finally starting to change. Today

Marcy came over and I told her what's been happening. She said, "Oooh, bummer." We spent most of the day in my bedroom trying to think up ways to stop Stanley. I suggested we kill him. Marcy said that was stupid — we'd end up in prison and get the electric chair, and neither one of us would look good in frizzy hair. So we thought some more, but no good ideas came. We're going to meet again tomorrow.

Tonight I did the dishes all by myself. Stanley stuck his tongue out at me and laughed. At this point I'm almost willing to risk frizzy hair.

July 20
Dear Diary:
Today was the worst day yet. Jeremy Hurlbut called and asked if I would like to go to the show with him. I would rather have stuck needles in my eyes, but of course I didn't say that. I just said, "No, thank you," and hung up. When Mom asked who called I told her it was a wrong number. Boy, was it ever. After that I hid in my bedroom until Marcy showed up. We spent an hour discussing ways to get back at Stanley. Marcy decided he should be hurt. Not seriously, of course, but enough to let him know I meant business. I asked what she had in mind. She pointed to Cuddles, who was curled

up on the end of my bed, and said, "Is there any way we can teach your old dog to bite?" I shrugged. "Probably, but we'd have to get him some teeth first. He's only got about five in his whole mouth, and they're loose." We'll have to think of something else. Marcy left a little while later, but she promised she'd keep working on it. Tonight at supper Stanley wrote *F.F. + J.H.* in his mashed potatoes. I got so mad I dumped my milk on him, and Dad sent me to bed without any supper. I cried forever.

They love Stanley more than they love me. They'll have to be punished too.

July 21
Dear Diary:

Stanley and I had a big fight this morning. Stanley wanted me to polish his shoes, and I told him to drop dead. He said he'd count to three, and if I didn't start polishing he'd call Margaret Crampton. One . . . "Go ahead," I said, trying to pretend it didn't matter anymore. Maybe I could bluff Stanley into backing off. Two . . . He started walking toward the phone. "See if I care. I really don't, you know," I lied. Three . . . He grabbed the receiver, and I grabbed his shoes and polished for dear life. So much for bluffing.

I'm getting desperate. This afternoon I saw Jeremy as I passed his house on my way to the library. He was sitting on the front porch petting his dog. Timber was growling as he ate something. It was either a chicken bone or a finger — I couldn't be sure which. Jeremy stopped me and asked if I wanted to go uptown with him for a banana split. I wanted the earth to swallow me up. "No, thank you," I answered quickly. "I'm going away." "Oh? Where?" he asked. "Peru." Tonight Stanley forgot to let Cuddles out, and he messed on the floor downstairs. I had to clean it up with a clothespin attached to my nose. Stanley smiled. I am his prisoner.

July 22
Dear Diary:

At last the tide has turned. This afternoon when Marcy came over we got sidetracked from our mission and started helping Mom sort through some old pictures. I was looking in a photo album and there it was — the artillery I needed to fight Stanley! The secret weapon that would let me fight fire with fire. I slipped the picture and its negative out of the plastic sleeve and hurried Marcy downstairs to my bedroom. When she saw the picture and I told her what I was going to do with it, she laughed so hard she fell on the bed, on top of Cuddles. I smiled too, but it wasn't a smile of humour. It was a smile of satisfaction. With this picture I can crush Stanley, now and forever. Victory will finally be mine. I will take no prisoners.

July 23
Dear Diary:
V-Day. Place: the kitchen. Plan: the final assault. I had made myself a scrambled egg and toast. Just as I was about to sit down and eat them, Stanley grabbed the food from under me and prepared to devour it. I jabbed him in the hand several times with my fork and told him to drop it. He did, then went to the phone, presumably to call Margaret Crampton. "Freeze!" I cried, whipping my secret weapon out of my pocket. He took one look at the picture and almost fainted. It was a photo of him when he was five years old, lying on the rug in front of the fireplace — naked! He screeched, snatched the picture from me, and ripped it to shreds. But I just stood there and laughed. "That's not the end of it," I told him. "I have the negative and I know how to use it. Mention one word of your lies to Margaret Crampton and I'll get plenty of copies made. I'll put your name on them and pin one to every bulletin board

in the city." Stanley saw I wasn't kidding. He was trapped. He had no choice. He slumped into a chair, defeated.

July 24
Dear Diary:
Tonight Jeremy Hurlbut called again and Stanley answered the phone. Jeremy asked if he could talk to me, but Stanley told him he doesn't have a sister named Frieda. I smiled. Victory — the taste is sweet!

4

The Bathroom That Frieda Built

There are many things about our house that I like.
We all have our own bedrooms and mine is the
farthest from Stanley's. The television in the
living room is positioned at just the right angle so
I can sneak peeks at it during meals. And the
kitchen counter isn't so high that I have to use a
chair to get on it when I snoop through the cupboard for the chocolate bars Mom hides up there.
What I didn't like about our house was that there
were five people living there, and we had only one
bathroom.

If you're the youngest in your family you'll
know what I'm talking about. The youngest is
always the last to get into the bathroom. Last
winter Dad made a rule that since there are so
many of us and so little time for us all to get ready

for school or work, each of us could spend only fifteen minutes in the bathroom. Unfortunately, once school let out and Margot and Stanley discovered they could spend all day in there, I couldn't even get in with a reservation.

"Margot," I shouted as I banged my fist on the bathroom door until it hurt, "what are you doing in there so long?"

There was a gigantic splash followed by a long gurgle of water. It sounded like she was diving. "I'm raising the Titanic," she replied. "Like, what do you think I'm doing? I'm having a bath."

"But you've been in there for two hours, and it's almost lunch time!"

"So? I have to get ready for this afternoon. Mark's coming over."

"Well, when do I get to have a bath?" I demanded.

"What day is today?"

"MARGOT!"

Stanley calls Margot the Creature from the Black Lagoon because she practically lives in the tub. But then Stanley shouldn't talk. He spends just as much time in the bathroom as she does, only he does it just to pester me.

Sometimes he locks himself in the bathroom just because he sees me coming to use it.

"Stanley!" I shouted once. "Open up! I gotta go to the bathroom!"

"What's the password?"

"You jerk! Open up!"

"Nope, that's not it. You got fifty cents?"

"I gotta go to the bathroom!"

"Go find a litter box."

"Stanley!"

I finally got so mad at both of them I told Mom and she called a family meeting. Dad calls them powwows because Mom is always smoking at them — smoking mad, that is.

"Why are you two always hogging the bathroom on Frieda?" she demanded that night, staring at Margot and Stanley.

They swallowed hard and shrank back. I love to see them squirm. But it didn't last long.

"Hogging it!" Margot sniffed indignantly. "What do you mean? I spend, like, only four hours a day in there, max! Is that so terrible?"

"I know of jail sentences that are shorter," said Mom dryly. "And you, Stanley? What's your excuse?"

He smiled smugly, which is the wrong thing to do when Mom is mad. "The door sticks," he answered. "I think it's from all the ozone breaking down or something."

Dad jumped quickly into the conversation before Mom could explode.

"So what happened to my fifteen minutes a person rule?" he asked. "Just because it's summer vacation do you think you can ignore it?"

Margot rolled her eyes in her head and groaned. "Oh, Dad, that's not long enough," she said. "School was one thing, but a date is completely different. If I don't get at least three hours to make myself up I'll look like . . . like Rat Woman!"

"You already do," Stanley put in, and we both broke up. Sometimes he can be really funny.

Dad immediately got between him and Margot before World War III broke out. "All right, Margot," he said patiently, "since you're the one who seems to need the bathroom so much, maybe you'd like to tell me what you think we should do?"

She thought for a moment. "We need, like, a schedule or something," she said, and got out a pencil and paper. She quickly drew up a plan, then, smiling triumphantly, handed it to Mom and Dad. It looked like this:

MARGOT FARKAS'S BATHROOM AND
BEAUTY SCHEDULE
7:00 - 9:00 A.M.:   Margot bathes.
9:00 - 10:00 A.M.:   Margot chooses outfit
                      and dresses.

10:00 - 11:00 A.M.: Margot applies makeup
 and does hair.

Mom's face went white. "Just when do the rest
of us get to use the bathroom?" she asked.

"There's, like, lots of time before seven," said
Margot.

"Only if we get up at three!"

Mom was already ripping up Margot's beauty
plan when an idea suddenly hit me. "Why don't we
build a new bathroom?" I blurted out. Everyone
stared at me.

"A second bathroom?" mumbled Dad.

"Yeah," I said. "Marcy Mae Peterson's mom and
dad built one in their basement a little while ago
and Marcy says it's the greatest. Why don't we
build one?"

I decided not to mention the trouble the Peter-
sons had had when the plumbers accidentally
broke the water line. They almost ended up with
an indoor swimming pool.

"What a wonderful idea!" exclaimed Mom.
"Heaven knows we certainly could use another
bathroom around here. Richard, let's do it!"

So it was decided that we would build a new
bathroom. Construction started almost immediately. At first Mom wasn't too keen about Dad
doing the work himself. She says he's about as

mechanically-minded as Snow White. And even though I don't say anything, I kind of agree with her. Once I saw him open a can of tuna fish with a crochet hook and a pair of manicure scissors.

But Dad said the job would be a piece of cake. And since I had come up with the idea, he appointed me official foreman. I thought that was great. It meant I could boss Stanley around as much as I liked.

The first thing we had to do was choose a space in the basement for the new bathroom. We finally settled on a spot near the stairs, close to my bedroom. Cuddles usually has his accidents there, and Dad figured that must be a good omen.

Then we started to build.

It took us a couple of days to put up the walls. That was really exciting! I got to hand the tools to Dad and Stanley, plug in the cords, and hold things. Once Dad let me hammer a few nails, but I kind of made a mess of them. Stanley said I hammered like lightning — I never hit the same place twice. I told him to never mind, I could hammer any way I wanted. I was the foreman.

The next thing we put up was the ceiling. Dad called it a suspended ceiling, but that wasn't always true. One afternoon it fell in on Stanley. Dad thought he was really hurt, but Stanley said he was okay, the ceiling tiles just hit him on the head. Margot said that was, like, a good thing, 'cause there was nothing much to hurt in there.

After Dad got the ceiling back up we helped him install the sink and shower stall. Now, I'm not too sure how plumbing goes together, and I don't think Dad is either. He tried to solder the pipes with a blow torch, and set the wall on fire. It wasn't a big blaze or anything, just a smoldering black mark on the wall that went out really easily, but for the next couple of nights Mom wouldn't go to bed without the fire extinguisher.

The last thing we put in was the toilet. That was the most fun, especially the way Dad hooked it up. I don't know exactly what he did wrong, but for some reason whenever it was flushed water would shoot out of the bowl like a geyser. Stanley and I thought it was a riot. We called it Old Faithful, but Mom called it par for the course and handed Dad the mop.

The work continued for a couple more days. Then finally, two weeks later, the new bathroom was finished. And what a bathroom it was!

"Go on in, everybody," said Dad excitedly, ushering us in for the grand opening.

Mom, Stanley, Margot, and I all crowded into the little room.

"Are you sure it's safe, Richard?" asked Mom, eyeing the ceiling and the plumbing suspiciously.

"Of course it is!" He waited. "Well? What do you think?"

Even though I had helped build it, there was nothing like seeing the room finally done. It was wonderful! From the sink to the shower, everything was gleaming white and new. Mom flushed the toilet and quickly jumped back to avoid a soaking. We were all surprised when the water drained the right way.

"Primo!" proclaimed Margot, and everyone cheered.

"I hereby declare this bathroom officially open," announced Dad. "And since it was all Frieda's idea, I think she should be the first to use it tomorrow morning."

"Here, here," said Mom, applauding, and even Stanley and Margot joined in.

I was speechless. Me? The very first one to use a bathroom? What an honour! I could hardly wait.

All that night I dreamed of the long, luxurious shower I would have in our new bathroom. It would be terrific! No more pounding on doors. No more yelling at someone to hurry up. No more washing in cold water. I would finally be first for a change.

When my alarm clock rang the next morning I jumped out of bed and raced for the bathroom. All that hot water was just waiting for me to splash around in! I shivered with delight. But when I reached the door and turned the knob, it wouldn't budge. It was locked. Someone was in there!

I stared at the door, confused, then pounded on it furiously. "Who's in there?" I yelled.

The door opened a tiny crack and Mom peeked out. "It's me, honey," she said.

"But what's going on?" I asked, starting to blubber. "I'm supposed to be the first one to use this bathroom! You and Dad said so!"

"I know, Frieda," said Mom quickly. "And I'm sorry, but your dad and I slept in and we're late for work. I had to use this bathroom because Dad's in the one upstairs. If you just wait a minute I promise I'll be right out, okay?"

My heart sank to my toes. My dream of being first had disappeared as quickly as the puffs of steam that had escaped when Mom closed the door. I sighed heavily and walked over to the basement stairs.

"Some things never change," I grumbled. Then I sat down and waited.

5

The Hand-me-down Blues

In my family we don't scare easily. In fact, Margot, Stanley, and I can sit through *The Thing That Pulled Out Its Eyes*, parts I through VI, and still have enough nerve left over to watch Mrs. Zykonsky down the street eat an egg salad sandwich without her false teeth. But that's not saying we're completely fearless. Oh, no. Each of us has one thing that's guaranteed to send us diving under the bed.

What are those things, you ask? Well, certainly not skinless people or slime or anything like that. They're just simple sentences. Margot's is "There's a zit on the end of your nose." Stanley's is "Margot is going to drive." And mine is "Frieda can always wear it."

Now I'll admit that, to a lot of people, wearing hand-me-down clothes isn't the most terrifying experience in the world. But if you'd ever had to wear my sister's hand-me-downs you'd know that it can be. You should see some of the things Margot has given me. Why, I'll bet my closet knows more horror stories than Stephen King.

There was a time when I didn't mind wearing Margot's clothes. But that was before she started dressing like the Bride of Ozzy Osborne. Now she's into statement dressing — you know, clothes that only go with pink and green hair. And when she grows out of, or more often gets bored with, her statements, guess who they get passed on to?

The last straw finally came the other day when she and Mom walked into my room with another castoff.

"You want me to wear that?" I blurted in disbelief. On my bed they were laying out a purple sack dress with the word *Megadeth* spray painted on the back. The colour was so bright I was sure it must be radioactive. "No way!" I declared. "I refuse to wear that rag."

"Rag?" sniffed Margot. "Like, what are you talking about? Don't you realize this is a genuine Kanipshun?"

"Sure is," I agreed whole-heartedly. "And that's what I'm going to start throwing if you keep giving me these rags!"

At those words my sister planted her hands on her hips and gave me that look I just hate — the one where her eyelids flutter and seem to jack up her top lip until her whole mouth turns into a sneer. Then she said, "Like, what turnip truck did you just fall off of? I was talking about the designer, you zod."

As if I was really supposed to care. I mean, the guy could be royal longjohns maker to the Queen for all it mattered to me. But no, trust Margot to use it to try to make me look dumb. Obviously she hadn't looked at herself lately — she's the one with green hair! She was just lucky Mom was in the room, because I was so mad I felt like pulling it out by its pink roots.

Mom must have noticed my cheeks turning red. She quickly jumped in to referee. "Now, Frieda," she said, "the dress isn't that bad. It's a beautiful shade of purple, and it's very popular this year."

"Maybe on Mars," I agreed. "But not with me. I'm not wearing it."

"Oh, come on," said Mom firmly. "You know as well as I do that any clothes you kids grow out of that are still in good shape go to the next oldest. It's a rule."

"Then make Stanley wear the dress," I said. "He's older than me."

Mom stared. A small blood vessel above her right eye was beginning to throb. "Frieda, you're being ridiculous," she said carefully.

"Of course she is," piped in Margot. "Like, anyone can see Stanley doesn't have the legs for a dress like that."

"But it's just not fair," I moaned, plopping down on my bed.

"What's not fair about it?" asked Mom. "Until Margot was thirteen, she had to wear your cousin Sharon's hand-me-downs. Now let's have no more of this nonsense. You're wearing the dress."

I was furious, but I knew there was no point in arguing any more. Actually I wasn't sure who I was more angry at: Margot for having the revolting clothes, or Mom for making me wear them. All I knew was I was sick of being treated like a little kid. When were they going to realize I was too old to wear hand-me-downs and quite capable of picking out my own clothes? Oh sure, I'm only eleven, but I'm a mature eleven. When Margot was my age she was so stunned. All she did was play with dolls and chase boys. Come to think of it, she still hasn't changed much. I'm not like that at all. Why, I haven't played with a doll in, well, over a month. Can't Mom see I'm almost a woman?

After a few days, when I'd had a chance to cool

off, Margot and I started talking again. She told me the reason I didn't like wearing her clothes was that I didn't have any style. Well, how could I? I told her. She got to pick out everything.

But Margot was insistent. She said it didn't matter what anyone wore, it was how they wore it that counted. This was really wild coming from my sister — a girl who is always on Polyester Alert and faithfully yells, "Man your lighters!" whenever she finds any. Nevertheless, she said she could really help me. With her talent she would, as she put it, "transform this rat child (me) into the bodacious Eurobabe that's inside and dying to get out."

Eurobabe? Me? I thought about it. Maybe Margot was right. Maybe I would like her clothes more if I had a look that was right for me. And besides, Marcy's birthday party was tomorrow night. Iggy Birdsell was going to be there, and I wanted to look extra good. I could never get him to notice me before, but maybe this time if Margot helped . . .

"Sure, why not?" I finally agreed.

"Faaabulous!" said Margot.

The next day right after lunch Margot went to work. All afternoon she shuttled me back and forth from the bathroom to my bedroom. She curled and teased and primped and painted me, never once letting me look at myself. She stripped my closet and made me try on outfit after outfit, only to make me change again and put on something different. Finally, about fifteen minutes before I was supposed to leave, she finished. Excitedly she herded me with my eyes shut tight to the big mirror in Mom and Dad's room for the grand unveiling.

"Okay, you can look now," she announced.

I did. For several long seconds I just stood there staring at myself, speechless. No matter how hard I tried I couldn't make my tongue work, mainly because I didn't know what to say.

It wasn't that I looked bad. Well, not really bad, because I didn't want to scream or anything. I just didn't look like me. But when I glanced at my sister I could see who I did look like. Margot had turned me into a carbon copy of herself. Not only was I wearing a pair of her jeans with metal studs all over the legs, but now we had the same hairdo too — something that looked like it had been done with a mixmaster. The only difference was that mine was tinted blue.

Hesitantly I touched my head. "Oh, Margot," I said. "I look . . . I look . . . "

"Bodacious!" she finished.

"But my hair is blue! Are you sure this is the look for me?"

"Like, totally," she reassured me. "Besides, the

colour washes right out. Now just relax. Tonight you're going to knock 'em dead."

I looked in the mirror again, hoping it wouldn't really go that far.

When I got to Marcy's the reaction to my make-over was just what I had thought it would be — mixed. Most of them thought I was Margot, and all of them disliked it.

"My gosh, what happened to you?" asked Marcy when we were alone at the refreshments table.

"Oh, Margot wanted to turn me into a Eurobabe, and I stupidly let her," I mumbled. "What do you think of my hair?"

"It's . . . it's nice," said Marcy guardedly. "In a Don King sort of way."

"You're telling me," I said. "If these studs didn't hurt my behind so much I'd sit down and have a good cry. Do you think Iggy's gonna notice me?"

"It's pretty hard not to," Marcy said. "Why don't you go over and find out?"

Slowly I walked over to the stereo where Iggy's back was to me as he put another tape in. Most of the girls thought Iggy was a nerd because of his greasy hair and his thick pop bottle lens glasses. But I thought he was kind of cute in an oddball sort of way. I took a deep breath and said, "H-hi, Iggy."

He turned to me and blinked several times. "Oh,

hi, Margot," he said. "Gee, I didn't know you were into birthday cake and party favours."

"I'm not Margot," I said, deflated. "I'm Frieda."

Iggy took off his glasses, wiped them on his shirt, and put them back on. "Frieda?" he repeated. "Boy, you sure look . . . different."

"Yeah, I guess," I said. I rubbed my clammy hands nervously on the fronts of my legs. "Do you like it?"

He took another look at me, this time starting from my head and working down. When he got to my jeans, he stopped suddenly and slapped his forehead as if he'd just remembered something. "Ah, geez," he said, "I forgot to take the snow tires out of the trunk of the car."

"What?" I asked, confused.

"My dad bought snow tires on sale," he explained. "He told me to take them out this morning, but I forgot. Your pants are a good reminder. Thanks."

My face instantly turned beet red. I had to get out of there before I started crying. "Don't mention it," I mumbled, and hurried away. I was so mortified I hid out in the bathroom upstairs until Marcy's mom threatened to get a jaws-of-life and break down the door.

When I got home that night Mom and Margot

were waiting up. Margot pounced on me as I walked into the living room.

"Well, how did it go?" she asked.

"Let's put it this way," I snapped. "You would have had a great time. I had an awful one."

"What do you mean?" asked Mom.

"Well, look at me," I said. "Thanks to Margot, everyone thought I was her. And thanks to you, Iggy Birdsell said my pants reminded him of snow tires."

"Me!" said Mom. "What did I do?"

"You said I had to wear them! I might as well give up my social life now and become a nun until I'm thirteen!"

"But Iggy Birdsell!" squealed Margot, grossed out. "Like, who'd listen to that geek anyway?"

I knew Margot was only trying to make me feel better, but sometimes she can be so dense. "I would," I said. "I like him, or shall I say I *did* like him?"

Mom gave Margot a withering look.

"Oh, sorry," said my sister. "I didn't know."

Well, I made a decision as a result of that night. The whole mess was my mother's fault. If she hadn't made me wear Margot's clothes I probably would have had a great time at the party. Instead I got humiliated. So I decided I wouldn't let her do that to me again. I wasn't going to wear anyone else's clothes anymore, and no matter how hard Mom tried there was no way she could make me.

For a whole week I managed to get by with the few everyday things I had of my own. Then disaster struck. Iggy Birdsell's mother called and invited me to a surprise birthday party she was having for Iggy on Saturday night. Would I come?

Since I didn't have anything decent of my own to wear, I had to say no. It was the hardest thing I've ever done. I knew this could have been a turning point in my relationship with Iggy, but I decided if I couldn't go looking like the person I wanted to be, I didn't want to go at all. There was a principle at stake.

The whole thing could have become one of the greatest tragedies ever told, and I really hoped Madonna would play me in the movie version. But then Marcy opened her big mouth and told Mom what I had done.

The afternoon of the party Mom found me moping in my bedroom. She sat down next to me on the bed. "I hear it's Iggy's birthday today, and there's a surprise party for him tonight," she said.

I didn't reply. I hoped my silence made her feel all guilty and yucky inside.

"I also heard you're not going," she continued. "Is it true?"

I nodded slowly.

"How come?"

I mustered all my courage and looked her in the eyes. "Because I have nothing to wear," I said clearly.

Mom glanced at my open closet. "Your closet looks quite full to me," she commented. "I'm sure you can find something."

"But they're not mine!" I blurted. "They're Margot's. I'm not going anywhere if I have to keep wearing her clothes!"

There, I had said it. I prepared for the bawling out I was sure would follow, but to my surprise Mom said gently, "Frieda, what's wrong?"

"Wh-what do you mean?" I asked.

"Something tells me it's not the clothing that's really bothering you. There's something else. What is it?"

Suddenly I felt like I was going to cry. I tried hard not to, but the lump in my throat kept rising higher and higher. Finally I couldn't hold back any longer. "I wish you'd stop treating me like a little kid," I cried. "I'm not a baby anymore."

Mom took me in her arms and held me close. "Frieda, am I doing that?"

"Uh-huh," I told her. "I just want to look like me for a change. Is that so bad?"

"No, it isn't," she answered, and her voice sounded kind of sad. "I guess you're growing up faster than I wanted you to."

I looked up and saw her eyes were shiny. "Why?"

"You're my youngest," she said slowly. "The last of my babies. When I see you growing older I know I am too. Sometimes that's a little scary. Maybe one day if you have children you'll understand. But you're right. You're not a baby anymore. You're a young lady, and it's time you had your own things."

It felt so wonderful to finally hear her say that. And yet part of me felt sad too, because I did understand. For a long while I just sat there in her arms, and as angry as I had been with her, I couldn't remember a time when I had loved her more.

6

A Girl's Best Friend

The idea came to me at breakfast. I was sitting at the kitchen table playing with my soggy Cheerios and trying to figure out how I was going to spend another boring summer day. Dad was going through the morning paper and muttering curses at the paper-boy. He was in a pretty bad mood. Not because it was morning or Monday or he had to go to work, but because the paper-boy had tossed the newspaper in a big mud puddle at the end of the walk and Dad had had to fish it out with a coat hanger.

"You know, this wouldn't happen if we had a decent dog," he grumbled as he tried to turn a page. It fell apart in his hands.

Mom, who was busy glaring at Stanley as he made his usual breakfast (last night's leftovers buried under two slabs of bologna and a big gooey gob of Cheez Whiz), glanced over at Dad. "Now, Richard," she said, "don't go blaming Cuddles for that kid's poor aim."

"Yeah," added Margot from the kitchen counter. She was hunched over her makeup mirror trying to get her hair to stand on end. "It's not his fault."

I turned and looked at Cuddles. He was lying on his back in a basket by the stove, fast asleep. His skinny legs were poking straight up in the air, and his toes were wiggling in time to his dreams.

"No, I mean it," insisted Dad stubbornly. "This wouldn't have happened if Cuddles knew how to fetch. Why, look at the Taylors' dog down the street. They have her so well trained the paper doesn't even have a chance to hit the ground before she has it in her mouth and is taking it in the house."

No one could dispute that. Compared to other dogs like the Taylors' Sheba, Cuddles did seem pretty useless. I mean, all he knew how to do was chase cats and sleep like a dead cockroach. But I never thought that was so bad. After all, there are plenty of dogs who can't even do that. I was sitting there thinking about what Dad had said and the long boring day ahead of me when suddenly the idea hit.

"If you want, I could train Cuddles to fetch," I announced.

Everyone turned and gawked at me like I had just stepped off a spaceship. They always do that whenever I come up with a good idea. I think they're just jealous 'cause they haven't thought of it first.

Stanley started to sputter. "You!" he blatted with as much disgust as I had for the slop he was eating. "What do you know about training animals?"

"Lots!" I said, which wasn't a total lie. "I've seen *Circus of the Stars* too, you know."

"Oh, don't be such a dork! It takes more than that. A trainer has to be smarter than the animal!"

"Well, that counts you out, doesn't it?" I retorted, and Dad quickly intervened before I put Stanley in a Ninja ear hold.

"Now, Frieda," he said, trying to calm me down, "I think what Stanley means is that it wouldn't be easy for you to train Cuddles."

I looked at him in disgust. "Great. You think I'm dumber than Cuddles too."

"No, no, honey," he said, patting my hand. "You're much smarter than Cuddles. It's just that he isn't young anymore. You might have a little trouble training him to do anything at this stage of the game. He's at least ten years old. He might be beyond learning anything new."

"That's right," added Mom. "He's set in his ways,

dear, and there's an old saying, 'You can't teach an old dog new tricks.' We wouldn't want you to be disappointed if it didn't work out."

Stanley saw his chance and beamed smugly. He had Cheez Whiz smeared on his teeth. "See, I told you!" he crowed. "You'd be wasting your time."

"Well, it's my time!" I shot back. "And that's how I'm going to spend it! I'm going to train Cuddles."

As soon as Mom and Dad had left for work I called up Marcy and invited her over. I told her I had this radical plan I needed help with, and she immediately snapped up my offer. It was either that or stay home and help her mom clean the bathrooms.

"We're going to do what?" she demanded when I gave her the details.

"We're going to train Cuddles. We'll teach him how to fetch and roll over and do lots of cool stuff like that. Who knows? Maybe we'll train him so well Walt Disney will give him a show of his own. Don't you think that's a fabulous idea?"

Marcy slowly came out of her trance. "Do you think we can do it?" she whispered doubtfully.

I shrugged. "*I* think so, but my parents aren't so sure. They think Cuddles is too old to be trained. He's ten, and they say you can't teach an old dog new tricks."

Marcy studied Cuddles, who was now wandering around the kitchen sniffing out crumbs that had strayed from the breakfast table. "Nah, he's not too old," she decided. "Why, my mom just got my little brother to stop wetting the bed, and he's eight. Cuddles is in his prime for learning."

This thought cheered me immeasurably, and Marcy and I went to work.

The first thing we did was go to the library. Since our own knowledge on training a pet was a little sketchy we wanted to flesh it out by seeing what the experts had to say.

The library is a super place to go if you want to find out about something. Ours has shelves jam-packed with how-to books on training everything from goldfish to scuba divers. For a second I toyed with the idea of seeing if they had anything on training stunned brothers, but then I decided Stanley was beyond any kind of help. We finally located two books on dog training to sign out. Then we hurried back to my place to read.

"It says in here," I quoted to Marcy when we were sitting in the kitchen with our noses in the books, "some dogs have naturally occurring talents that don't show up in any other breeds. They're called genetic traits."

Marcy looked up and frowned. "What's a genetic trait?"

"Well," I thought for a moment, "I'm not too sure. But I think it's like Stanley and my cousin Bernie. They're both jerks. It runs in the family, so I guess it's a genetic trait."

"Oh."

"Yeah." I referred to my book again. "It also says that Shetland sheepdogs and border collies have in their genetic makeup a natural instinct to herd. This instinct makes it easier for their trainers to teach them how to tend sheep and cows and stuff like that. Irish setters are the same way, only their instinct is to fetch."

We both looked at Cuddles. He was lying in his bed again, only this time his bum was propped up against the wall and his head hung down to the floor. He opened his eyes and stared back at us.

"Do you think there's any Irish setter in Cuddles?" asked Marcy.

I shrugged. "Maybe." His hair *is* long, and it's sort of reddish in colour; but his body doesn't look much like an Irish setter's. Instead of being tall and lanky, he's built more like a bullet — short and stocky, with a head that comes to a blunt point at the nose. Dad always says he's part mole, but I know that's dumb. Cuddles hates the dark.

Marcy and I continued our research for a few more minutes, then she snapped her book shut and announced that she was sick of reading. To tell the truth, I was too. We decided we were ready to start training.

We took Cuddles and the books outside to the backyard and developed a plan of attack. Since organization is the key to any project's success — or so Mrs. Crowell always said — we decided to start with the simple stuff like leading and sitting, and work our way up to the more complicated tricks.

We sat Cuddles down on the grass and prepared him for his first lesson — leading. Since I didn't have a proper leash we stole the plush belt off Margot's bathrobe. I tied it around Cuddles' neck, taking special care to make sure the knot wouldn't slip and choke him.

I looked at Marcy. "Okay, now what?"

She glanced in her book. "It says to tug on the leash and say, 'Come.'"

A simple enough command, I thought. I looked back at Cuddles and did as I was told. He just sat there, staring at me.

"Maybe he didn't hear you," suggested Marcy.

I called him again and pulled a little harder. He lay down. Finally I jerked on the leash and yelled, "Cuddles, will you come on!"

This time he freaked out. He jumped up in the air like an overgrown grasshopper and howled and thrashed his head against the leash. When I tried to take it off him the real crying broke out.

"Oh, for Pete's sake, Frieda, stop bawling," ordered Marcy. "You have to be firm with him."

"I-I can't!" I blubbered. "He's scared. I'm scaring him and now he hates me!"

"Don't be so silly! You have to be firm. He'll calm down. That's the only way he's going to learn. Now try to lead him again."

I wiped away my tears and followed Marcy's orders. This time, to our complete amazement, Cuddles gave up fighting and followed. I walked slowly around the lawn, and he followed attentively at my side.

"Oh, my God, Marcy, look!" I squealed. "He's doing it. He's doing it! I'm actually leading him!"

Well, I was for about five seconds. Then our neighbours' cat strolled down the alley, and Cuddles started leading me. He tore off across the yard, nearly ripping my arm from my shoulder. Marcy and I finally rounded him up five blocks away.

When we brought him back we decided to forget about teaching him to lead for a while. My arm couldn't take any more of it. The next thing we concentrated on was sitting and staying on command. Cuddles took to that idea about as well as he had to leading.

According to the books, I had to push his bum on the ground and say 'stay,' repeating this word as I walked away from him. It seemed like an easy thing to get Cuddles to understand, but when I tried it he sat for a moment, then followed me across the lawn.

"No, Cuddles, sit!" I said, pushing his bottom back down and walking away. "Stay." He rolled over and fell asleep.

"He's just not understanding you," observed Marcy.

"Well, what do you suggest?" I asked.

"Here." She got down on her hands and knees beside Cuddles. "You tell me what to do, and I'll show him how it's done. Okay, tell me to sit."

I felt a little stupid saying it, but if she was game, so was I. "Sit, Marcy," I commanded, and she obediently dropped her bum to the ground. "Stay," I ordered, slowly backing away from her. She sat in position and watched me intently. "Okay, come here," I said, and Marcy trotted across the grass on her hands and knees. "Good dog," I praised, and patted her head.

We both looked back at Cuddles to see if he was catching on. He was sitting up now with his head crooked to one side as he watched us.

"I think he's beginning to get the picture," Marcy

said. "Let's do it again." She got on her hands and knees and we repeated the performance. But after twenty demonstrations it was painfully clear that the only one learning anything was Marcy. She was getting so good at the trick that I was sure Walt Disney would give her a show of her own. But Cuddles just sat there snapping at the flies that were dive-bombing his head.

"We're doing something wrong," I remarked on our lack of progress. "Maybe we should try what I read in my book — find his natural instincts and work on them."

Marcy stopped brushing the grass from her pants and gave me a tired stare. "And what are those?" she asked. "All he knows how to do is chase cats and sleep."

"Yeah," I agreed glumly, kicking at a dandelion growing in the grass. Then an idea struck me. I wheeled around and looked at Marcy again. "That's it," I told her. "Cuddles can chase cats, and chasing is half the job of fetching. Quick, let's get a ball!"

We hurried to the garage and found an old tennis ball in a box of junk. Then we went back outside, and I held it in front of Cuddles' face.

"See the ball?" I said, moving it slowly in front of his cloudy eyes. "See the ball? Go get it!" I tossed it toward the hedge.

Cuddles perked up his ears and watched it bounce across the lawn. I quickly retrieved it and tried again.

"Okay, Cuddles, watch the ball. Watch the ball. Doesn't it look like a kitty? Go get the kitty!" I threw it again. This time Cuddles stood up and wagged his tail as he watched it fly through the air. My heart leaped, and Marcy gave a sharp squeal of excitement.

I brought the ball back once more. This time for sure he'll chase it, I thought confidently. I held the ball right up to his nose. Cuddles sniffed it intently and looked at me. "Fetch it, boy! Fetch the ball!" I yelled, and threw it. Cuddles lay down and went to sleep.

Marcy and I groaned and crashed to the ground beside Cuddles. As we sat there mulling over our predicament she pulled out the box of Smarties she always keeps in her back pocket, and we divided them up.

"You know, Frieda," she said, crunching loudly on her candies, "this is hopeless. No matter what those stupid books say, we're never going to train Cuddles."

As much as I hated to admit it, I was beginning to think the same myself. I nodded sadly and popped another Smartie in my mouth.

"He's too old to learn anything new," she went on. "Let's face it, your parents were right."

Cuddles suddenly caught a whiff of chocolate and sat up. He looked at me with such sad, wanting eyes that I fed him a Smartie. He gulped it down in one swallow and jumped on me, begging for more. I glanced over at Marcy and giggled.

"You know why you can't teach an old dog new tricks?" I asked her.

She shrugged.

" 'Cause he knows them all already!" I fell back in the grass laughing, and Cuddles licked my face hungrily.

7

Creatures

In science class my teacher told us there are many creatures of habit in this world. "Mammals, fish, insects and birds are all such creatures," he said. "In fact, any living organism that displays repetitive behaviour is a creature of habit." He was talking, I suddenly realized, about my parents.

Like salmon swimming upstream to spawn or swallows returning to Capistrano, my parents do a number of things on a regular basis. For instance, every night Dad wanders through the house shutting off lights and muttering, "I'm gonna die a poor man." And at mealtimes Mom can make hollering for Margot, Stanley and me to come to the table sound like the first act in *Carmen*. They've done these things (and others) for as long as I can remember. It's part of what makes them seem normal to us.

But one night something different happened. Something drastic. I'm sure Mom and Dad felt they were taking a giant step for mankind with it, a step that would revolutionize parenting. I felt they had lost their marbles.

"Suuuuuup-perrrrr!"

Mom was in rare form that night. Her voice easily blasted through the latest Janet Jackson video blaring from the television set. I started to get up, but just then George Michael came on singing "I Want Your Sex." I sat back down. The spirit was willing, but the flesh was weak.

"Suuuuuuuup-perrrrrr!"

"Where are my green shorts?" called Margot from her bedroom.

"In the laundry basket," Mom hollered back.

"You mean you haven't washed them yet?"

"I haven't had time. Everyone get to the table!"

"But I need them!"

"Wear the white ones."

"I hate the white ones!"

"Go naked. No, forget I said that!"

"Where's Stanley?" yelled Dad.

"Suuuuuuuuup-perrrrrrrr!"

The back door slammed.

"Where were you, young man?" demanded Dad.

"Out."

"Doing what?"

"Nothing."

"Then why weren't you in here? You know it's supper time!"

"I was busy."

"Go and wash up!"

"SUUUUUUP-PERRRRRRR!"

"Margot, come quick!" I yelled. "George Michael is on!"

"George Michael is a has-been," observed Stanley.

"He is not!" defended Margot.

"Is too!"

"You don't know what you're talking about. He's — "

"Hurry up!" I interrupted. "You're gonna miss him."

"Look, this is your last warning!" yelled Mom. "Shut off that television and get to this table!"

"Now!" added Dad.

"We're coming," I answered obediently, but Margot and I didn't move one millimetre from the couch and the lust of our lives.

When the video ended we strolled into the kitchen in time to meet Stanley entering from the hall. As usual Mom and Dad were standing by the sink, arms folded and teeth clenched. Steam was rising from the dishwater behind them, or maybe it was from their ears. I wasn't sure.

"Well," asked Margot brightly, "what's for supper?"

Instead of tearing into their usual speech #38, *Mealtime Tardiness: The Primary Cause of Parental Stroke*, Mom calmly went to the table, picked up the big bowl sitting in the centre, and held it on display. "As you can see, it was chili," she said crisply. "Please note the purplish scab that has formed on top. Chili with a purplish scab is no longer just chili, but ice cold. Thank you, my children, for making this past hour of cooking after a particularly hard day at work so rewarding." Then she turned and walked to the garbage can. Dad solemnly opened the lid, and to our amazement we watched our supper slide into the bag with a wet, icky splat.

"B-but what are we going to eat now?" sputtered Stanley.

"You can lick the wax buildup off the furniture for all I care," snapped Mom. "Your father and I are going out for supper. Fend for yourselves!" With that, she and Dad stormed out of the house, slamming the back door behind them.

"Geez, what's her problem?" I asked.

"PMS?" volunteered Stanley. Margot glared at him.

"What's PMS?" I asked.

"Pretty much stressed," answered Margot dryly.

"Dad too?" I asked.

"Dad too. Someone get the milk. I'll get the corn flakes."

I don't think I had ever seen Mom and Dad so angry with us. Cripes, they didn't get that upset the time I forgot to tell them I invited forty-two of my closest friends for a sleepover the same weekend we were getting the toilet snaked. Or the time the house was black with flies, and they discovered that Stanley had been hiding his school lunches under his bed. Or even the previous Tuesday when they had to shut the power off and cut the phone lines to get us to come to supper.

Two hours later Mom and Dad returned, but unfortunately their good humour hadn't. The second they stepped into the house they called a powwow. We all gathered around the kitchen table.

"Children," said Dad as if he was announcing a death in the family, "there is an attitude problem in this house."

"Like, you're not kidding!" said Margot indignantly. "What's the big idea of throwing our supper in the garbage? We could have starved."

Mom lunged at Margot, but Dad pulled her back. "I was talking about your attitude, not ours," he said.

"Our attitude?" repeated Stanley. "What did we do?"

Mom lunged at Stanley, but again Dad pulled her back. I didn't say a word. I was sitting closest to Mom; there was no way Dad would get her off me in time.

"We're fed up with the way you children treat us," Dad explained.

"You tell them, Richard," said Mom, spurring him on.

"You seem to think the only reason your mother and I are here is to be your personal slaves," he continued. "Well, we're not. We work hard all day while you guys do absolutely nothing. We're sick and tired of your indifference, your glib remarks, your sheer laziness. We have rights too, you know. And until you've learned to respect them, we're not lifting another finger for you. When it comes to the cooking and cleaning, the washing and ironing, you guys are on your own!"

The news hit the three of us like a ton of bricks, or one of Margot's cakes. Margot and Stanley made gurgling noises, then finally managed, "Y-you can't do that! That's child neglect! We'll call social services!"

"The phone's on the wall and the number's in the book. Do you want me to dial?" offered Mom.

Utter silence. They had us, and they knew it.

"That's what I thought," said Dad. "Before we adjourn, your mother and I want to leave you with one last piece of advice. The number for Meals On Wheels is also in the book. Good luck, my children. You're going to need it."

Self-sufficiency — what a concept! For a while Margot, Stanley, and I wandered around the house like we had just been handed death sentences. How could Mom and Dad do this to us? We weren't ready for such a big step. Why, we had just stopped eating with our fingers! And now we were expected to cook? Incredible! As a last resort we met in my room and tried to figure out what we were going to do.

"We're gonna die," prophesied Margot. She was lying on my bed, staring at the ceiling. "I can already see next week's headlines in the *National Enquirer.* 'Teenagers Devoured By Vacuum Cleaner.'"

"Look, maybe we're overreacting," I said. "Maybe this won't be as hard as we think."

"Are you kidding?" said Stanley. "I overheard Mom and Dad whispering. They figure we'll last three days. Four if we keep our fluids up."

"Well, maybe it'll be different if we organize ourselves," I suggested.

"What do you mean?" asked Margot.

"I mean we divide up the work load. One of us can do the cooking, someone else can do the cleaning, and the other one'll do the washing and ironing. That way each of us can concentrate on one job instead of four."

Margot's face lit up. "Awesome plan, Frieda!" she said. "So, like, how are we gonna decide who does what?"

I shrugged. I couldn't be expected to think of everything.

"I know!" said Stanley suddenly. "My guidance counsellor once told me that before undertaking any job a person should take a hard look at himself and find out what his natural talents are."

"Well," said Margot slowly, "like, I can make toast."

Stanley and I started bouncing with excitement. "Excellent!" he said. "You can do the cooking."

"I know how to start the vacuum cleaner. I'll do the cleaning," I volunteered.

"And because I know how to get the dirtiest, I'll do the washing and ironing," said Stanley. "Oh, you guys, this is going to be a piece of cake!"

The next day we went to work. Since this was such a big occasion for us, I decided to keep a record in my diary.

Day 1:
Got up this morning and found Margot planning today's menu. I wanted to see it, but she wouldn't let me — said it was a surprise. Then Stanley announced he was going to do the laundry. Margot and I told him he'd better read the owner's manual first. He said he already had. Translated, I figured that meant he had opened the cover and glanced at the pictures. I was right. An hour later we all had splotchy pink underwear. Margot suggested Stanley be put to sleep. Motion carried.

Noon. Lunch was a surprise, all right. In three hours all Margot had come up with was bologna sandwiches — toasted. I hate bologna. I tried not to let on, because Mom and Dad were home. I just said, "My, isn't this fancy?" But when I gagged halfway through, they snickered. They're jealous, I can tell.

After lunch I vacuumed. I started in Mom and Dad's room and accidentally caught their bedspread in the power nozzle. Got scared and called Margot. It was wrapped in there so tightly we had to cut it out. Now there's a big hole in the middle of Mom and Dad's bedspread. Covered it with a pillow and hoped they wouldn't notice.

Supper. Margot surprised us again. She made wieners, in other words, bologna in a tube. Mom and Dad had fried chicken — my favourite. I stared at a drumstick so long I thought it was whispering to me. Decided to go to bed and listen to my stomach growl. I hope tomorrow is better.

Day 2:

Got yelled at this morning. Mom noticed the hole in her bedspread. She said I was going to have to pay for it. Each week she'll deduct two dollars from my allowance. I'll be seventy-eight by the time it's paid off.

At noon I walked into the kitchen and found Margot standing over the toaster with a fire extinguisher. I asked her where lunch was, and she said it went to live with Jesus. Just as well, I thought; we were having bologna again. For lunch I had two stale crackers.

In the afternoon I did a little house cleaning. Could only work for an hour though — I tripped over one of Stanley's dirty socks, and it bruised my foot.

For supper Margot made bologna roll-ups. Stanley and I almost threw up. She had taken slices of bologna, spread grape jelly on them and . . . well, *bon appetit*. Stanley asked if she would make something else, like soup. Margot told him no, she'd broken the can opener trying to figure out how it worked.

I'm starving. Before I went to bed I took out the Bible. I wanted to be closer to God before the end came. I opened it, and the first line I read was, "Man cannot live by bread alone." I wrote a letter to the Pope. Asked if he would add bologna to that list.

Day 3:

The end is near. This morning I woke up to the smell of smoke. At first I thought it was Margot burning my corn flakes. Then I discovered it was Stanley ironing. He was burning the sleeves off our shirts. Now we have lots of vests.

Later I decided to clean the downstairs bathroom and had my first encounter with a hair ball. Noticed the sink was draining too slowly. Told Stanley. He suggested I plunge it. After three good pumps, out plopped this big hairy glob. Thought it was a dead rat and started screaming. I'll never be the same again.

At 1:32 the end came. Margot saw what Stanley had done to her favourite sweatshirt and threw a mondo-hyperspasm.

"You bonehead!" she screeched at him. "What did you do to it? It's no bigger than a facecloth!" She held it up, and I thought she was being generous.

"I guess I forgot about it in the dryer," said Stanley with a shrug.

"For how long? Two weeks?"

"Well, how was I supposed to know it would shrink?"

"Like, who can wear this now?"

"Barbie and Ken?" I suggested.

"Very funny," she snapped. "Look, guys, I don't know about you, but I've had it. God, by the time school starts I'll have nothing to wear but pyjamas!"

"That's if we don't conk out first from living on bologna," Stanley put in.

"All right, it's settled then," Margot declared. "We've got to get Mom and Dad to take care of us again."

Motion carried. Later that afternoon when Mom and Dad got home we called another powwow. I'm sure they both knew what it was about, but they pretended to be surprised just the same.

"Mom, Dad," started Margot slowly, "we have something we want to tell you." She looked at Stanley and me for support, and we both nodded vigorously. "We want to apologize for the way we've treated you. Over these past couple of days we've discovered it's not easy doing this household stuff and — well, we're sorry for taking you for granted."

Tiny smiles played at the corners of Mom and Dad's mouths, but they fought them off and remained very serious. "Your apology is accepted," Mom said quietly after a short pause.

Margot, Stanley, and I breathed a heavy sigh. "Excellent," I said. "Does this mean you're going to take care of us again?"

There was a moment of silence before Mom said, "No, it doesn't."

Our mouths fell open like trap doors. "What?" squeaked Margot.

"It means we'll help you," clarified Dad. "But you're still going to be taking care of yourselves."

"But we can't!" wailed Margot. "You've seen what a disaster we are at it."

"That doesn't matter," said Dad. "The more you do it, the better you'll get. Besides, you have to learn sooner or later. Or do you expect your mother and me to do everything for you for the rest of your lives?"

I looked at Margot and Stanley and they looked at me. The idea had real merit.

"Let me rephrase that," said Dad quickly. "Your mother and I have just broken a bad habit we had. Let's not start it again, okay?"

"Oh, all right," we agreed reluctantly.

"Great!" said Mom. "Now, everyone up to the stove. It's time for your first cooking lesson."

The three of us grumbled loudly as we got up from our chairs. Parents might be creatures of habit, I thought, but sometimes they're just creatures.

8

How To Ride With Your Parents: A Guide To Family Travel

Our neighbours always ask my parents what their secret for a happy family trip is. Every time we get home we all appear so calm and relaxed they wonder if we're not taking something. Dad always sticks out his chest and laughs, "No, no, no drugs. We're just a special kind of family. We know how to travel together." I think it's a result of the exhaust fumes that leak into the back seat from the hole in the car floor.

For as long as I can remember my parents have felt that the family that rides together, sticks together. If you ever get the chance to ride in our car you'll realize we have no other choice. The shocks are so bad that if we don't hang on to each other we'll become human pinballs.

I estimate I've taken approximately four thousand car rides with my parents since I was born. One day I decided this was far too many. I felt if I was ever to have peace of mind again I'd have to cut down. But my parents soon talked me out of it. They said, "Get in that bloody car, Frieda, and stop acting so stupid!"

Right then and there I realized that as a child I have few rights in this world, and none at all in Mom and Dad's car. So I decided to do something about it. The following is a survival manual composed from the years of bitter experience I've gained travelling with my parents. I offer it to you in the hope it will in some small way make your summer-time family trips a bit more bearable.

The Vehicle

The first and perhaps most important factor in any trip is the vehicle. If you're going anywhere it always helps to do it in a decent car, not something that looks like it should be pulled by a cow.

My parents' station wagon is the latter kind of vehicle. It's embarrassing to ride in. The roof and hood are brown. They match the rusted out fenders and doors. The front seat is permanently locked in the forward position, which is great for Mom, but if Dad wants to drive he has to wrap his legs around his neck just to get in, then untangle them under the steering wheel. The visor on the passenger side falls at will, endangering the head and hands of anyone foolish enough to tinker with the radio. The glove compartment opened in 1984 and hasn't closed since. The back seat has two types of springs — those that are broken and those that poke you in the behind. The upholstery is ripped, the engine knocks, and the muffler drags on the ground — what's left of it, that is.

At best, our car is a heap. Stanley calls it the Road Warrior, and in a way that name almost suits it. I definitely feel like I'm going into battle every time I get into it.

Vehicle Maintenance

The trick to having a decent car is not always fiddling with the engine, but knowing when to leave it alone. The Farkas family car wouldn't be half bad if certain people, namely Dad and Stanley, would learn to keep their hands off it. Riding in an old beater is bad enough, but riding in a souped up old beater makes the mind spin.

Mom keeps a chalkboard on the refrigerator on which she writes a thought for the day every morning. For the past five years the same message has always appeared: "Dear Richard and Stanley: If it's not broken, don't fix it." Any day now she's going to spraypaint that message onto the car.

It's not that Dad and Stanley don't know what they're doing when they fix something. Well, okay, it *is* because they don't know what they're doing. To watch them work on the car is like watching a blind man do brain surgery. Once, they decided the ignition wasn't working properly. For three days they adjusted and readjusted everything from the air intake hoo-hahs to the floor mats. When they were finished we had the only car on the block that had to be started by the five of us taking turns blowing on the end of a hose.

Companions

The next area you should take a good hard look at is your travelling companions. Rule number one: Pick a seat beside a person you like. If you don't, you'll live to regret it. Mom is always telling Margot and me, "You can't choose your relatives." We know you can't. But you *can* choose the person you're going to sit beside in an enclosed space. In most families kids fight over who gets to sit by the window. In our family we fight over who has to sit beside Stanley. It's not that Margot and I don't like him; it's just that we choose not to seat ourselves next to a person who picks his nose for hours at a time and then offers to brush that piece of lint from our lips.

Boredom

Perhaps the number one killer on any family trip is boredom. Since my parents, like most others, aren't that crazy about hand-to-hand combat in the car, Margot, Stanley, and I have developed a list of activities guaranteed to make time fly. Now I'm not talking about dopey games like "I Spy" and "Count the Cow." I mean fun games like the following:

"Heat Out": This game is entertaining — and easy to play! All you need is a functional heater, rollable windows, and several willing victims. To play, you roll up the windows, seal the vents, turn on the heater and wait. The first person to complain or faint from the heat is proclaimed King of the Weenies for the remainder of the trip.

"Ear Lobe Lottery": Guessing games are always fun. To play Ear Lobe Lottery simply bet money on how many hairs your dad has in his ears, then count them. The hairs, that is. Winner takes all. Oh, by the way, just count the black wiry hairs — those skinny fair guys are too hard to keep track of.

"Restroom Roulette": This game is sure to take everyone's mind off any trip. All that's needed is a long, desolate stretch of highway — the Coquahalla or anywhere in Death Valley is always nice. Upon entering the highway sing out, "I gotta go to the bathroom!" Chant this until your parents actually reach a gas station or pull off to the side of the road. Announce then that you no longer have to go. When they ask what you mean, shift in your seat slightly, smile mysteriously, and quickly roll down the window. A guaranteed scream.

"Backseat Biology": Why shouldn't trips be educational? Steal your brother's comb from his back pocket and try to identify all the different life forms caked on it. Dandruff is like snow — no two flakes are alike. To make things a little more interesting, suddenly shriek that you saw something move. But be prepared to defend yourself. Chances are the next thing to move will be your brother's fist.

"Curler Crafts": Busy hands are happy hands. One of the quickest ways to kill boredom is to occupy your hands and mind with handicrafts. One of my favourites is something called Curler Crafts. Locate your mom's makeup bag and use her hair curlers — the Velcro ones, the others won't work — to make interesting and useful things like ashtrays or drink holders. Decorate with pins. May I suggest that you work quietly at this activity? If your mom is anything like mine, she won't take kindly to watching her curlers become the framework for a canoe.

Rules and Regulations

When it comes to developing activities to take the boredom out of travelling with your parents, the only limit is your imagination. But as with any activity, there are certain rules and regulations that you as a passenger and child must follow. I will leave you with a treasured few that I have learned along the way:

1. I don't understand it either, but when it comes to music parents hate Guns n' Roses. They'd much rather listen to some zod named Wayne Newton. I mean, who is this guy, and why does his hair drip more oil than a leaky tanker?

2. Never stand up in your seat. It's too dangerous. Parents are sure to notice you attempting to give your brother a judo chop to the throat if you stand up to do it. Lie back and use your feet the way I do.

3. Parents leaning back in their seats trying to sleep do not want flies crawling around on their faces. Even if you've ripped the wings off.

4. Never rub pencil lead on the eye cups of the binoculars, then hand them to your mom and ask if that's a moose you see in the distance. In all likelihood she won't see either the moose or the humour.

5. Perhaps the most important rule to remember is moderation in all things. Know your parents' breaking point and respect it. If, after 203 rounds of "Ninety-nine Bottles of Beer on the Wall," that tiny vein above your dad's left eye turns black and starts to throb, cool it. You're probably getting close to that limit.

9

Babes in Boyland

"You won't believe the date I had last night. He was gorgeous! He made Jon Bon Jovi look like Danny DeVito. And you'll just die when you hear what we did!"

What? What? I wondered. Could anyone be better looking than Jon Bon Jovi? Impossible. And what would that broomhead be doing with him anyway? Marcy and I nearly fell off our bench straining to hear more.

The two of us were spending an ordinary boring Tuesday afternoon sitting outside The Wizard's Castle, the video arcade and general hangout in the mall, listening to the girls in the buffalo stance. We call them that after an excellent song by Neneh Cherry. They were mostly grade nine headbangers who even looked like cows as they stood endlessly chewing their gum and swapping the dirt on just about everything. They met here every day, and whenever Marcy and I didn't have anything better to do we'd hang back and try to listen in. Some days it was better than Oprah!

Today the topic was dating. Carrie Levitt was giving the rest of them the scoop on the hot date she had last night. But, as usual, by the time she got to the juicy part her voice had dropped to a whisper, and the other girls were huddling close around her. Marcy and I craned our necks and strained our ears in an effort to catch any little tidbit that might float our way. But, as usual, we never heard a peep.

"Geez, I hate it when they do that to us," muttered Marcy. "Just when they're getting to the good part too. It's not fair!"

At that moment a sharp gasp came from the girls as Carrie's story reached the good part. It seemed to rise up like a rain cloud from a steamy jungle floor and then burst, showering them with pure delight. Five of them were left so weak they had to lean against the wall for support. The rest just stood by muttering over and over, "Awesome . . . totally awesome!"

I looked at Marcy. "Well, it must have been pretty good," I commented dismally.

"Oh, Frieda," she groaned. "I'm so jealous I could scream!"

We watched as the group straggled off toward the Orange Julius counter. When they had all disappeared into the crowd Marcy let out a long dreamy sigh. "Can you imagine how exciting it would be if we could go out on dates too?" she breathed.

I certainly didn't need much prompting. This summer was turning out to be the most boring one I could remember. "Boy, can I ever," I sighed just as dreamily.

Then Marcy turned with a look I've grown to know and dread. "Well, why don't we?" she demanded.

Before she had even finished speaking a thousand reasons had popped into my head, all of them supplied by my parents. The main one was that we were too young. They have instructed Margot, Stanley, and me, "Over our dead bodies will any of you start dating before the age of fifteen!" To them it's one thing to have a boy friend and hang around together like Marcy and I do with Kevin Lagori and Jeffrey Carlson, but it's quite another to have a boyfriend and go out on dates. They feel that before the age of fifteen no one is mature enough to understand the responsibilities of having a boyfriend and dating. And now that Margot is fifteen I can see them wishing they had set the limit at sixty-five.

"You know our parents would freak," I reminded Marcy. "They think we're too immature."

"Well, we're not," she declared. "Why, just since the beginning of summer I feel like I've matured a lot. If it keeps up I'm sure I'll be wearing a bra next month. Besides, they don't have to know about it, do they?"

I thought for a second. It certainly wouldn't be the first time we hadn't told our parents about something we did. "I-I suppose not," I said. "But who would we get to take us out? We don't have any boyfriends."

"I'm sure Kevin and Jeffrey would do it."

"Kevin and Jeffrey?" I looked at Marcy hard. "You're kidding, right? They're not our boyfriends."

"So who said they had to be?"

"But you're supposed to really like a boy before you go out on a date with him," I pointed out.

"Well, we do really like Kevin and Jeffrey, don't we?"

"Yeah . . . but that's different. I think you're supposed to be in love."

Instantly Marcy's freckled face pulled into the

sourest grimace. It reminded me of nutrition night at her house, when her mother serves liver and parsnips. "Foul!" she sputtered. "Are you sure?"

"That's what I heard on *Degrassi Junior High*."

"It can't be true," she decided. "I'm sure Carrie isn't in love with all the guys she dates. Cripes, she changes them oftener than most people change socks, and look at all the fun she's having."

"And look at the reputation she's got," I said bluntly.

"Look, it's not going to hurt anything if we just do it once," said Marcy coaxingly. "Besides, I'm sure a couple of dudes like Kevin and Jeffrey would just die if they got a chance to go out with a couple of babes like us. C'mon, what do you say? Let's do it!"

I still wasn't sure. It just didn't seem right. But then Marcy came up with the winning argument.

"Do you want to just sit around here for the rest of the summer and be bored out of your skull," she asked, "or do you want to have the most totally awesome time of your life?"

Well, since she put it that way . . . "Okay," I said. "Let's go tell them."

For the next half hour we searched the mall for Kevin and Jeffrey, but no matter how hard I tried I just couldn't get as excited as Marcy about this date. For one thing, I had no idea what eleven-year-olds were supposed to do on a date. For another, it was impossible to imagine Kevin and Jeffrey as dudes. Dorks, yes, but dudes? Now, don't get me wrong — they're great to hang around with. But would you go out on something as important as your first date with two guys who like to wear space helmets with quivering eyes on the ends of the antennae and carry plastic laser guns that make screaming noises like prehistoric birds? I don't think so.

Marcy finally caught sight of the boys by the fish tanks. They were following a couple of old ladies with blue hair, and from the looks of it, monitoring them for radon emissions.

"Hey, you guys! Wait up!" called out Marcy.

The boys stopped and looked at us, then raised their arms high in salute. "Greetings, aliens!" they intoned in unison.

Marcy groaned with embarrassment, and I quickly glanced around to see if anyone was staring. "Geez, do you guys have to do that in public," muttered Marcy as they came up to us.

Jeffrey shrugged. "There's nothing else to do."

"Sure there is," she told him excitedly. "Frieda and I just came up with this terrific idea. You two are going to take us on a date!"

Kevin and Jeffrey looked at each other, then Jeffrey ordered, "Phasers on stun. Fire when ready." In less than a second we were toast.

Marcy quickly slapped their guns away. "Knock it off," she said. "I'm serious. You guys are going to take us on a date. Kevin, you're gonna take Frieda, and Jeffrey, you're gonna take me."

Kevin scowled. "On a date? Why?"

"Because they're a riot," said Marcy. "We'll have loads of fun."

"And just what makes you think we want to go out on a date with you two?" asked Jeffrey suspiciously.

Good question, I thought, looking at Marcy for help. In a flash her expression turned as innocent as a lamb's, and she very meekly said, "I don't know. We just thought you'd want to, that's all. But I guess everyone was right. You aren't grown up enough for something as important as this. C'mon, Frieda, let's go and find somebody more . . . mature."

We turned to leave, but Kevin quickly stopped us. "No, wait! We're mature. We'll go out with you."

Marcy looked at them again, this time scrutinizing them through eyes narrowed to slits. "Are you sure?" she asked. "We can't have boys for this. We need men!"

Kevin and Jeffrey swallowed hard and nodded as if their heads were attached to springs. "We're sure," said Kevin.

"Excellent," said Marcy. "Isn't that excellent, Frieda?"

It always amazes me how Marcy can suck them in like that. She says it's something she's learned from watching her mom. Mrs. Peterson calls it using her feminine wiles. Mr. Peterson calls it a dirty rotten trick.

"When do you want to go?" asked Kevin.

Marcy turned to me and I shrugged. "Let's see," she said thoughtfully. "How about tomorrow at one?"

"Make it two," said Jeffrey. "I've got violin lessons at one."

"Two o'clock it is."

"So where do you want to meet?" asked Kevin. "I don't think either of our parents are going to let us have the car."

"No kidding," said Marcy. "How about we meet right here?"

"Okay," agreed the boys.

"Anything else?" asked Marcy.

Kevin and Jeffrey were silent for several long seconds, then Jeffrey said shyly, "What do you want to do on our date?"

"Surprise us," said Marcy tiredly. "Geez, do I have to do all the thinking? Just make it good, and for heaven's sake leave those ridiculous helmets at home. You're men now!"

"Right," said Kevin.

"Right," said Jeffrey.

"Oh, brother," said Marcy, and we left.

All the way home I couldn't help worrying. I wondered if maybe our parents were right, maybe we were too young to be dating. None of us knew anything about it, and I certainly had a lot of questions buzzing in my head. Questions like, since Kevin and Jeffrey weren't really our boyfriends, was it all right to let them pay our way? And what if—and I was really worried about this—they wanted to kiss us? Should we let them?

I would have liked to talk the whole thing over with Mom and Dad, but I knew if they even suspected what I was up to they would turn Catholic just so they could send me to a convent. I would have to get my advice from Margot.

Margot was going with a new guy named Rat Tail. His real name was Larry Kiminski, but nobody dared call him that. The only words he knew were grunts, and his idea of dressing up was changing the clothes on the little plastic doll that hung from the safety pin in his ear. I'm quite certain Rat Tail would have been history around our place if his dad hadn't been my dad's boss, but at least Margot was dating. She might be able to give me some tips. I really couldn't trust her not to tell Mom and Dad what I was planning though, so that night I told her about it in terms of "a good friend wants to know." She was happy to give my mythical friend plenty of advice, but after I'd heard it I wasn't sure how good it was.

First she told me there was nothing wrong with letting the boys pay our way. In fact, it was a rule with her. A girl's got to have standards, she said. If a guy wanted to go out on a date with her, it was gonna cost him. (Between you and me, I think she got that from Joan Collins on *Dynasty*.) As for the kissing part . . . well, she just told me to trust my instincts, they'd tell me what to do. In theory that sounded great, but how could I trust my instincts when I wasn't even sure I had any?

At two o'clock the next afternoon Marcy and I stood nervously by the fish tanks waiting for Kevin and Jeffrey. We had decided to dress up, so we had brought our good clothes in a tote bag and changed in the washroom at the mall. The rest of our stuff was in a locker for safekeeping. Even if I do say so myself, we looked pretty bodacious.

But when we saw Kevin and Jeffrey we got a

real shock. They were awesome! Maybe it was because we had forgotten what they looked like without their space helmets. They had on new torn jeans and ripped T-shirts, and I thought it was really nice of them to dress up too. They even wore aftershave. It stung our eyes a little when they got close, but it smelled great from a distance.

"You guys look excellent," I greeted them.

"Thanks," said Kevin shyly. "So do you."

"So what are we going to do?" asked Marcy. "Did you guys decide on something?"

Jeffrey gave Kevin a nervous glance, then said, "We thought we'd start by taking you to Wonder World."

"Great," said Marcy. "Let's go."

As we walked to the amusement park at the far end of the mall I could see that Kevin and Jeffrey were just as nervous about this as . . . well, as Marcy and I were. But it was an excited kind of nervousness. Even though we had all been to Wonder World at least a thousand times before, today felt as exciting as the very first time. After all, we had never been here like this — on a real date.

By the time we got to the park and started going on the rides, we began to relax. Kevin and Jeffrey bought a big book of tickets, and for the next couple of hours they took us on one ride after another. It was great! Marcy screamed so much she went hoarse, but no one minded since she usually talks too much. My favourite ride was the Drop of Doom — a cage-like box that takes you about ten storeys straight up and then lets you fall all the way back down. The ride took less than five seconds, but Marcy and I needed at least half an hour before we stopped wanting to throw up.

To make us feel better we went over to one of the side venues, and Kevin and Jeffrey won us each a stuffed animal by beating gophers with rubber hammers. I got a brown mouse and Marcy got a red one. They were really nice, but it sure took the boys a long time to get them. Since neither Kevin nor Jeffrey have that great eye-hand coordination they ended up paying about triple what it would have cost if they had bought the mice in a store.

In spite of that, I realized our date was working out really well. I couldn't remember when I had had so much fun, and I felt kind of dumb for being so worried about it. The four of us ate tons of junk food and laughed and chased each other, and then something really amazing happened. When we were getting off the Gravitron Kevin took hold of my hand. At first I thought it was just so he wouldn't fall down because he was so dizzy. But after a while he was walking straighter and he still didn't let go. I glanced back at Marcy and saw her and Jeffrey doing the same. I guess Margot was right. My instincts must have kicked in then, because I didn't let go either.

Around four-thirty Kevin and Jeffrey announced they were going to take us out to dinner. I really thought that was too much. They had already spent a lot of money on us, and besides, it was getting late. Marcy and I would be in for it if we weren't home by six. But the boys were insistent. They said they wanted to make this date one we would always remember. So, not wanting to disappoint them, we agreed.

We walked down to restaurant row and went into a really great pizza place we knew. We ordered a humongous pizza, but none of us ate much; we weren't very hungry. Instead we talked and laughed some more, especially when Kevin made a portrait of our principal in the leftovers.

Then Kevin and Jeffrey's wish came true — our date turned into one we would never forget. The bill came, and it was for $23.75. At first Marcy and I didn't have a clue anything was wrong. We just sat there pigging out on the accompanying mints while Kevin and Jeffrey dug into their wallets and counted out money. It wasn't until they stopped at $8.61 that we knew we were in big trouble.

"Wh-what's the matter?" I asked. I knew full well what it was, but I had to hear it from them to believe it.

Jeffrey and Kevin didn't say a word. They just sat there staring at their empty wallets and making tiny whimpering noises.

"I don't think they have enough money," whispered Marcy numbly.

"Do you have enough money?" I asked the boys. This time their whimpering was faster and more high-pitched. I took it to mean no.

"Oh, my God!" gasped Marcy. "What are we going to do? I left my wallet at home."

"So did I," I added.

"Oh, my God!" said Marcy again. "We're gonna go to jail!" And she started to cry. "How could you pinheads be so stupid and spend all your money?"

Jeffrey came to himself and snapped, "Well, you morons helped us spend it!"

"We did not!" yelled Marcy. "Did we force you to stand there and beat gophers all afternoon until you were broke? You might as well have cut your money up for all the good it did."

"Yeah," added Kevin, "especially the stuff we spent on you!"

By now everyone in the restaurant was staring at us. But our yelling stopped abruptly when the waiter walked over.

"Is there a problem here?" he asked coolly.

At first no one would look at him, let alone say anything. Finally I spoke up. "Uh . . . uh, yes, sir," I said. "Y-you see, sir, we don't have enough money to pay our bill."

His eyebrows shot straight up. "Oh. That is a problem. I'll have to get the manager."

He left, but in a few seconds he returned with a short fat man with a drooping black moustache.

When I explained our predicament to the manager he didn't seem too upset. At least he didn't go call the police, which is what I had expected. Instead he gave us a very stern talking-to about how people who eat and don't pay their bill are just like shoplifters. Then he said he was going to call our parents.

As far as Marcy and I were concerned a firing squad would have been better. We begged him not to call and asked if there wasn't some other way we could settle our bill. We knew we were pushing our luck, and from the look on the manager's face so did he. So we quickly explained that our parents didn't know we were out on a date and that we weren't supposed to be on one in the first place.

Suddenly he started to laugh.

"I guess I was young once too," he said, smiling. "Well, all right. We can settle this some other way. Years ago I used to make bad customers work off their debts by washing dishes in the kitchen. How about you stay here for an hour and see if you can put a dent in that mountain back there?"

Marcy and I could have kissed him. We nodded eagerly. I never dreamed I'd be so thrilled to wash dishes.

Then the manager turned to Kevin and Jeffrey. "What about you guys?" he asked. "Are your parents against dating too?"

The boys looked at us, then back at each other. "No, but we'll stay and wash dishes," they decided.

"All right. The kitchen is this way. Follow me."

For the next hour we worked like dogs. The water was scalding hot, and no matter how fast we worked, we just couldn't make any progress. We all took turns washing while the rest dried, and it seemed that for every dish we cleaned, three more were brought in to take its place. To top it off, the staff treated us horribly. Word of what we had done spread like fire, and several times I looked up to find the waiters and waitresses openly staring and snickering at us. It was so humiliating. I don't know which got redder, my hands or my face.

No one said much the whole time we worked. We were all too angry and embarrassed to say any more to each other than we had to. So when our hour was up I was surprised to see the boys walking back to our locker with us. I honestly thought they'd take off in the other direction and never speak to us again after what had happened. But they didn't.

Finally I broke the ice. "Thanks, guys, for taking us out. I had a lot of fun in spite of everything. And thanks for staying and helping us. I mean, you could have let the manager call your parents."

Kevin grinned shyly. "What are friends for, right?"

"Right," I said, smiling back.

"Does this mean you guys aren't mad at us anymore?" asked Jeffrey.

"Of course we're not," I said. "Are we, Marcy?"

Marcy glared at me. "Speak for yourself," she sniffed.

"Oh, come on. Is that any way to treat the guys after everything they did for us?"

"Did for us?" She blinked hard. "Are you nuts, Frieda? It's because of them that I've got the worst case of dishpan hands in the world!"

"Well, it wasn't all their fault," I pointed out.

"We were just as much to blame."

"We were not!"

"We were so. After all, this date was your idea. I tried to tell you we weren't ready yet, but you talked me into it. Remember?"

Marcy stubbornly clenched her jaw, but she knew I was right. After a few moments of deliberation she grudgingly admitted, "Yeah, I suppose so." She turned to the boys and said, "I'm sorry. I didn't mean all that stuff I said. I guess this was my dumb idea."

"Oh, it wasn't that dumb," said Jeffrey. "We had a lot of fun. In fact, I wouldn't mind if we did it again sometime."

"Really?" said Marcy, a little amazed.

"Really," said Kevin, then added quickly, "But how about we wait a while, huh? Like a few years?"

Marcy and I looked at each other and grinned. It was a date.

10

Song of a Sick Person

There's only one thing worse than getting sick on your summer vacation, and that's getting sick and having my brother and sister look after you. When it comes to illness there's one thing they both firmly believe: if you're sick, don't expect much sympathy from them. I know, 'cause I certainly didn't get any.

One morning I woke up feeling not so hot. It wasn't anything I could pinpoint, just a general punky feeling that seemed to stretch from the roots of my hair right down to my toenails. By noon my eyelids felt like Godzilla was dancing on them. By nightfall I had broken out in a rash.

I tore out of the bathroom where I had been examining myself and flew into the living room. "Mom! Mom! What's wrong with me?" I wailed as

I raced to the couch where she and Dad were sitting.

They both turned from the TV to look at me. Stanley, who was playing with Cuddles on the floor, sneered, "You're short, ugly and stupid. You want more?"

But Dad gave him a reproachful look, and Mom came to my side.

"What's the matter, Frieda? Why are you crying?" she asked.

In between loud sniffles I pulled up the back of my shirt and pointed to a patch of skin on my left shoulder. "Look, I've got spots!" I exclaimed. "They're all over my back, and there are some on my face and throat too, see? And they're itchy!"

Mom and Dad took me into the kitchen where the light was better so they could have a closer look. The commotion even drew Margot away from her telephone conversation for a second. She inched closer and peered at my back too. Suddenly she pulled away hissing, "Zits! Gross! Don't you dare use any of my Clearasil!"

Mom and Dad didn't seem convinced that's what it was though. They continued to pore over my blister-like spots as if they expected to read their fortunes.

"Well, what is it?" I asked impatiently. "Is it gonna go away?"

Dad put his hand on my forehead and asked, "Do you feel sick?"

I nodded and told him about my headache and the yucky feeling I'd had all day. Dad took his hand away and looked at Mom. "Loretta, she's warm. I think it's chicken pox."

That's all Margot needed to hear. She dropped the receiver, clamped her hand over her mouth and nose, and fled from the kitchen screaming, "If it's contagious I'm moving!"

Stanley was a little more understanding. He yelled from the living room to ask if I was going to die and could he have my room if I did? If he'd been any closer I would have belted him.

The next day a quick visit to our doctor confirmed Dad's diagnosis. It was chicken pox all right. The doctor prescribed seven days of bed rest for me at home. I couldn't believe it. Chicken pox, seven days of bed rest, and all on summer vacation! How could this be happening to me? No one's supposed to get sick on summer vacation, only on school days. What a waste!

But if you think I took the news hard, you should have seen Margot. She was downright ruined.

"Stanley and I have to do what?" she bleated when Mom told her they had to take care of me while she and Dad were at work.

"You heard me," said Mom. "Frieda's not that sick, but she's going to have to take it easy for a while. I want you and your brother to just watch out for her and make sure she stays in bed and is comfortable. Do you understand?"

Margot's face crumpled into a tortured mask. "But, Mom, that's, like, totally unfair! How can you expect me to be a . . . a serving wench? My nails won't take it. I have this aversion to all things gross and sickly!"

"Then how come you're still going out with Rat Tail?" countered Stanley. That was a mystery most of us couldn't figure out.

"Now, look," interrupted Dad, "we don't want to hear any more about it. You and Stanley are old enough to have a little responsibility around here. Your mother and I can't be in two places at once. While we're at work you two are going to take care of your sister, and that's that."

Margot gave me a searing glare. I got the feeling they were going to take care of me all right — permanently!

I realize in some families illness makes people come together, but ours isn't one of them. So often

I've heard about people who need organ transplants and whose brothers and sisters jump up and down offering them a kidney. On my first day in Margot and Stanley's care I was lucky if they gave me the time of day.

"Look, I'm sorry I got sick. But it's only chicken pox. Don't you think you're overreacting a little?" I said to Margot as I lay on the bed with my pyjama top pulled over my head. She was smearing some kind of pink lotion on my back with rubber gloves on her hands. The rest of her body was covered in a mask and gown she had made out of an old bed sheet. She looked like the mad doctor in some old horror movie.

Stanley was hovering somewhere in the background. He had Dad's video camera and was recording everything we did. The way he was using the zoom lens was making me a little nervous.

"I'm not taking any chances," grumbled Margot, pulling down my top and motioning me to get under the covers. "I've got a big date planned for this weekend, and I'm not going to let some spotty little brat ruin it for me."

Big date? I could just about imagine what she and that hood Rat Tail were planning to do. Probably rob a bank.

"Well, if I'm such a bother why don't you just

send me to a leper colony?" I retorted, fighting back my tears. I had read about those in *National Geographic*. They were special places you had to go if you had leprosy, and right about now I had a pretty sure feeling they'd accept people with chicken pox too.

"Don't give me any ideas," she told me, spraying a thick cloud of Lysol around her. In a swirl of bed sheet and disinfectant she and Stanley left, slamming the door behind them. It sounded like the hollow clunk of a cell door.

That first day pretty well set the tone for the rest of my recuperation. From nine until noon I lay in bed doing nothing but watching spots invade what little clear skin I had left. As far as I could count I had 378 blisters on my body. And they were multiplying at the alarming rate of five new ones per hour. If they continued at that speed I would look like a pizza before nightfall. No one visited me.

At lunch time Margot brought in a bowl of tomato soup and some soda crackers. Actually she didn't bring them in. She just set the tray outside my bedroom, knocked on the door, and ran. From one until two I scratched. From two until three I tried to visit with Stanley. I told him if he came down and talked to me I'd let him videotape the patch of spots on my side that was growing in the shape of a pumpkin. From three until four I got so bored I tried to escape from my room. Margot caught me watching TV from the living room closet and chased me back to bed. For the rest of the afternoon I sat alone in my room watching my fingernails grow and trying not to scratch.

At five-thirty relief finally arrived when Mom and Dad came home. Boy, was I happy to hear them. They came straight down to my room to look in on me. Mom put fresh lotion on my chicken pox, and it felt so much better than when Margot did it. Probably because Mom loves me and wasn't wearing rubber gloves. Then Dad asked how I was doing. I desperately wanted to tell him how terrible Margot and Stanley were treating me, but then I wondered what would be the use. Even if Mom and Dad did chew them out, I really doubted it would make them treat me any better. And from the tired looks on Mom's and Dad's faces I got the feeling right now wasn't a good time to complain about not getting along. Instead I said I was fine. I would just find some other way to handle Margot and Stanley.

The next morning I got an idea. On a tiny notepad I scavenged from my desk I started a special diary to record all the crummy things Margot and Stanley did to me. Maybe when they were brought to trial for my death the judge would accept it as evidence and send them to the electric chair. That thought gave me new hope. I called the diary "Song of a Sick Person," and kept it hidden under my pillow.

Day 2:

It's Monday, I think. I'm losing track of time. My condition is no better.

Had an awful night last night. The itching is driving me crazy. Every time I managed to fall asleep I dreamed I was locked in a room full of mosquitoes, wearing nothing but Margot's Strawberry Delight body lotion. Every time I woke up I found myself scratching. In the morning I told Mom about it, and before she went to work she suggested I wear gloves to prevent me from scratching the blisters open. Margot offered to get them, but then she said my winter mitts weren't in my drawer. Now I'm wearing Dad's socks on my hands, but I suspect Margot didn't look too hard.

Day 3:

No change.

Woke up crabby this morning. Stanley offered to get me a suppository. I offered to punch out his teeth. My hair is stiff with pink goop because I now have chicken pox on my head. I scared the paperboy when I looked at him out my window. My skin was breaded with lotion and bed lint and I felt like a battered shrimp. Margot finally relented and let me have a bath. Of course the water had to be ten thousand degrees so I wouldn't catch a chill. Afterwards she covered me with fresh lotion. Now I feel like a cooked, battered shrimp.

Day 4:

No fresh chicken pox, and the older blisters are starting to form scabs. Am I getting better?

Fought with Stanley today. I wouldn't let him look at my chicken pox with a magnifying glass, so he got all huffy and called me Scabby Abby. This afternoon I heard a noise upstairs and sneaked out of my room to investigate. I found Stanley and six of his idiot friends in the living room watching the videotape he took of me getting my back rubbed with lotion. They were all having a good laugh at how gross I was. I got so mad I broke the tape over Stanley's head. Later he came down to my room and apologized. He even gave me ten dollars — half the admissions he charged at the door. I'm still mad at him, but I'll put the money toward a good cause. Maybe a poisonous snake.

Day 5:

Most of the blisters have dried up. Asked Mom if I could get out of bed. She said no, not until the scabs fall off.

Was mega-bored today. I've read everything in the house, including the owner's manual to the blender. In a rare act of kindness Margot let me get out of bed and watch the soaps with her. I could only stand twenty minutes, then went back to bed. All that snivelling and carrying on — and that was just Margot! I think I'm losing my mind.

Day 6:

Some of the scabs are starting to fall off. The itching is gone. The end is near!

Marcy came over to visit, but her mom wouldn't let her come into the house. She said I could still be contagious. Instead we talked through my bedroom window — that is, until Margot made me close it. She said the fresh air would shock my system. I'd like to shock her system. Before Marcy left I stuck a note on my window. It read, "Pray for me."

Day 7:

Saturday. Mom is home, and she said my chicken pox are healed enough for me to get out of bed. Excellent!

Got dressed with such enthusiasm I almost broke a leg putting on my jeans. At last I'm healed! I'm gonna celebrate! I was forcing a comb through my hair when I heard a terrible scream from upstairs. I went to investigate and found Margot in the bathroom showing Mom something on her neck. It was a tiny red blister.

Margot took one look at me and screamed again. Chicken pox! I had ruined her date with Rat Tail!

Mom called Stanley and discovered he had broken out too. She sent them both to bed and asked me if I would help her take care of them. Of course I said yes. I was so happy I practically floated back to my room to finish combing my hair. While I worked a little voice in my head said, "Revenge isn't right, Frieda. Are you going to let their terrible treatment of you affect the way you take care of them?"

I chewed my bottom lip for a moment, then smiled. Well, maybe just a little.

11

The Last Laugh

The trick to surviving in my family is knowing when to laugh. A good sense of humour can soften any crisis. And did I ever need to remember that the day Mom told me to clean my room. If I hadn't started to laugh, I know I would have cried.

"You want me to clean my room?" I questioned between sputters of stunned laughter. Cold chills started to crawl up my spine like frozen spider legs.

"That's right," said Mom. She and Dad were busy putting away the last of the breakfast things before they went to work.

"Wait a minute, wait a minute," I said. "You mean you want me to *clean* my *room*?"

"That's what I said."

"My bedroom?"

"Yes."

"You mean the place where I sleep?"

"No, I mean the place where Cher sleeps. What do you think? Of course I mean your bedroom. I want you to clean it."

"Why?"

"Why?" I could tell from the way Mom was looking at me that she had only one nerve left and I was starting to get on it. "Because it's filthy, that's why! Your father and I are thinking of subletting it as a pig sty. Last night I tried to look in on you while you were sleeping but I couldn't. Something was blocking the door. I think it was a lint ball."

"Oh, Mom," I groaned. She always could exaggerate things.

"Don't 'Oh, Mom' me!" she warned. "Your bedroom is a disaster area! I'm surprised you don't have to tie a rope around yourself at night just so you can find your way out in the morning." A tiny smirk played at my lips, but I didn't dare let it go any further. The speech continued. "Frieda, you know your room is your responsibility. You haven't picked up a thing in there in the past six weeks, and I'm worried the Board of Health is going to step in. Just because it's summer vacation doesn't mean you can stop keeping your room clean, you know."

"But it's my room," I objected. "I like it messy."

I also must have liked playing with death, because at that moment Mom's finger stabbed the air, and she started waving it in front of my face as if it was loaded.

"Don't talk back to me, young lady!" she growled. "When you start paying the mortgage around here you can say you like a messy room. Until then I like it clean. Understand?" I nodded weakly. "Good. Now when I get home tonight I expect to find that bedroom spotless. And if it isn't I hope you've figured out some way to get out of your skin, because I'll have that instead!"

I looked at Dad for support, but he was nodding in agreement with Mom. I was all alone. "All right," I mumbled, and slunk off.

The trouble with having a dirty bedroom isn't living in it, like some people think. It's cleaning it. I mean, I could make my home on an earthquake site, but ask me to clean it . . . well, where do you start?

I guess my biggest problem is I'm a slob. I freely admit that, because I come from a long line of slobs — namely Margot and Stanley. But it seems I'm the worst. In fact, my room is known as the Temple of Doom, probably because on any given day it looks so bad only Indiana Jones would have the guts to enter it.

That day wasn't any different. As I slowly pushed the door open a tiny gasp caught in my throat. It's weird how you never really notice how bad something is until someone else points it out to you. Mom definitely was right. My bedroom was a disaster area.

In the far corner, just under the ceiling, stood a mountain of clothes. It had avalanched a couple of weeks ago and claimed the bed. It's a good thing I wasn't sleeping in it at the time. The only way I would have escaped was if a Saint Bernard had come in and dug me out.

Against the opposite wall was my dresser. I call it my shrine to junk. Not only am I a slob, I'm also a pack rat. Every little treasure I've come across during the last six years could be found somewhere on top of my dresser. Some of the more interesting items were my collection of pop cap liners that spell "I know you are, but what am I?" (I may win a trip to Disneyland with those), a pair of earrings in the shape of chewed bubble gum (come to think of it, they may *be* chewed bubble gum), my picture of River Phoenix, a stuffed pink flamingo, a sock my cousin found at a Stones concert (Marcy thinks it could be Mick's and considers it holy), and an old grilled cheese sandwich. I'm not sure why I was keeping the sandwich. It was either a snack I forgot about or an experiment to see how long fossilization takes. All my dresser drawers were pulled out and empty of clothes, but who needs drawers when you have a corner to pile things in, right?

My closet wasn't much better. The doors were in their usual position — open and waiting for my latest offering of books, magazines and the other assorted goodies I usually toss inside. The only clothes on the rod were my winter coats and ski pants. Come November, those too would be on the pile in the corner. And above, shivering on the edge of the shelf, was a pile of boxes and blankets. I must have stared at it too long because it suddenly toppled over, almost choking me to death on the dust.

As I stood there surveying my room, two hopeless questions whirled in my head: Where was I going to start cleaning up this dump? And how was I going to do it without the help of a bulldozer? Then I saw something. Peeking out from behind the dresser was a framed sheet of paper. It was Mom's ten commandments for keeping a tidy room. On the day she decided to go back to work she gave Margot, Stanley and me each a copy of that sheet. She said we had to learn it, follow it and hold it dear to our hearts, for she wouldn't have time to clean our rooms anymore. That was the saddest day of my life.

Now I walked over to pick the sheet up and read it again:

I. Thou shalt not wear clothes and cast them off wherever you feel like it. Clothes have feelings too. They do not like to be wadded into a ball and left in a heap. Learn, my children, to uplift them from the floor and hang them in the closet. Otherwise you will go through life naked.

II. Dressers are beautiful. Dressers cost money. Money your parents would rather use to go on luxurious vacations and buy fancy cars. Dressers do not like to be rammed with the vacuum cleaner, piled high with junk, or doused with cheap perfume until their varnish peels. Always remember, dressers embarrass easily. Never leave their drawers open.

III. Thou shalt not consume food or drink in bed and leave the dishes lying around. They always get broken. If they do, do not bring the pieces to me and tell me you have no idea how they got that way. I will know you are lying. The dishes will know you are lying. And sometime during the night those broken pieces will come back and get you!

IV. Sleeping on a bed is an act of civility. Civilized people make their beds every day. They do not use them as a place to store books, bags of chips, dirty underwear or chicken bones. Animals do this. Animals sleep on straw. Observe this rule and you may never have to know what it is like to sleep on straw.

V. Junk is nasty. Junk is evil! Do not hoard junk, hate it! Junk usually does not have arms or legs, so it has no way of getting to the garbage can. Be kind and help it along. Garbage cans are funeral homes for junk. Bid farewell to it there.

VI. Clothes hampers must be fed every day. If you do not put your dirty clothes in them, they will get hungry and be sad. Boo-hoo. Do not be afraid to feed them. Clothes hampers are gentle creatures. Clothes hampers are our friends.

VII. Carpeting likes to be seen. It is vain that way. It is happy when people walk on it and say, "My, what lovely carpeting!" Carpeting doesn't like to be covered with clothes, papers, dirt or food. If something is lying on the carpeting, pick, wipe or vacuum it up. If you do this you will be my favourite child.

VIII. The word "closet" comes from the Old French, meaning "a small room or cabinet for clothing, provisions and utensils." Do not confuse this with the words "storage shed." A closet can only hold so many things. Do not house anything in it that is larger than its door, needs eight hours of sunlight, or will spring out and snarl at your mother when she goes to look inside it.

IX. Lights require electricity. Electricity costs money. Money is something your father and I want to leave you when we die. Learn to turn off the lights whenever you are not in your bedroom, or go out and marry well.

X. Above all, do not hide things in your room. Especially food — perishable food. Hiding means you are trying to keep something from me. That is a secret. It shows you do not trust me. It's not nice to keep secrets from your mother, especially if she can smell one and for the life of her can't find it.

I sighed and looked around again. Well, Mom's list hadn't exactly told me how to clean my room, but it had given me a good idea of all the bases I had to cover. I grabbed a handful of coat hangers from the closet and, with those ten commandments in mind, began my attack.

The first job I hit was the pile of clothes in the corner. The amazing thing about piled clothes is that after a while they tend to grow together. I practically had to rip my socks, underwear, tops and pants apart to separate them. Then I put them into two piles — those that were clean and those that were dirty. The clean ones I hung up or folded; the dirty ones I just leaned against the wall.

I discovered another amazing thing too — clothes left in a pile will reproduce. Honest. At one time I had enough drawer and closet space for everything. Now it didn't matter how I arranged my stuff, the only way I would get it to fit was if I built onto the house. After a while I abandoned the leftover clothes on my bed and went onto something more important — lunch.

An hour later I returned to my bedroom and tore into the next job — my dresser. Mom defines junk as "that stuff which has no useful purpose and should be thrown away." I can't help wondering if she feels the same way about things in a museum. After all, this stuff was my history. I couldn't just pitch it. I decided to call her at work and tell her what I thought. She told me when people started paying her cold, hard cash to see a shrivelled cheese sandwich, then I could keep it. Until that time I was to live with a little less history or not live at all. Two hours later I had my dresser cleaned off.

Next I moved on to my closet. I sorted through all my games, books and puzzles and kept only those that still had all their parts, pieces and pages. The stuff that didn't went on the bed with my leftover clothes.

Then I vacuumed the floor and stacked all my shoes, pausing only twice — once to go to the bathroom and once to watch *Wheel Of Fortune*. I couldn't help myself there. Vanna was wearing a sequined Band-Aid.

Unfortunately I should have made better use of my time. Before I knew it five-thirty had rolled around. I was just finishing cleaning under my bed when I heard the sound of someone outside. My heart nearly stopped. Mom and Dad were home and I still wasn't finished!

Before I could mutter, "I'm toast," the front door opened and Mom yelled, "Frieda! I'm home!"

I looked at the big pile of junk on my bed and immediately knew what I had to do. I would hide it in the closet. That meant breaking commandment number eight, but better that than my neck.

I grabbed everything and stuffed it on the top shelf, praying Mom wouldn't find it. I had the door shut and was smoothing out the covers on the bed by the time she walked in.

For the first few seconds she stood in the doorway gawking around like a fish that had jumped out of its bowl. Finally she managed to close her mouth and try a few words. "Frieda?" she said slowly. "Did you do this?"

I nodded weakly. "Of course I had a little help," I said, pointing to her ten commandments where they now hung on the wall. I knew that would please her.

"My goodness, this room looks terrific," she said, and began a more detailed inspection. I moved in front of the closet in the hope that she wouldn't look there, but I didn't have to worry. When she had gone through the dresser and looked under the bed without finding any junk, she was so pleased she threw her arms around me. "Oh, Frieda, I'm so proud of you. You've done a beautiful job!"

I shrugged shyly and started breathing a little

easier. But suddenly a rumbling sound came from inside the closet. I froze. Mom looked around quizzically.

"What was that?" she asked.

"My . . . stomach," I said, and quickly held my belly. "I'm hungry. What's for supper?"

Before she could reply there was another rumble. This time it was followed by a bang as something fell onto the closet floor.

Mom looked around again. I had no idea what body sound could cover that noise. Then Mom motioned for me to step aside and flung open the closet door. Instantly she was showered with clothes, books and boxes — everything I was trying to hide.

A sock dangled from Mom's ear and she angrily snatched it away. "Frieda Farkas!" she shouted. "What do you have to say for yourself?"

I couldn't hold back any longer. "Look out below?" I giggled, then burst out laughing.

I howled and hooted as Mom grounded me for three days. Then she told me that since I thought that was so funny, I could clean out all the closets in the house. Guess who's laughing now. She left my room and went upstairs. I flopped down on my bed.

When was I going to learn? I thought in

despair. There's definitely one thing more important than knowing when to laugh, and that's knowing when not to.

12

The Fall of Summer

The end of summer vacation is always a sad time of the year for me. The days are shorter (there used to be enough sunlight after supper for Marcy and me to play five good games of "Kick The Can" with some of the kids on my block; now it's almost pitch black before we get in three rounds), the weather is much cooler, and the last day of summer vacation means the next one is — yuk! — school.

I've always hated school, especially the first day. Some kids think it's exciting. Not me. I find it too stressful. I mean, just when you get used to spending two glorious months doing whatever you want whenever you want, suddenly you're shoved into a strange room filled with semi-familiar faces and a sergeant-major for a teacher.

I think my basic problem is that I'm a worrier.

On any ordinary day I worry about lots of things. But when it comes to the first day of school I worry about everything. I worry about whether I'll hear my alarm clock and make it to school on time. I worry about how my hair is combed. Will I look like the other girls, or will I have gone out of fashion and look like King Kong's armpit? I worry about how the other kids will act toward me. Will they notice me? Talk to me? Like me? Or will they ignore me, sneer at me, hate me? I worry about failing arithmetic again and getting stuck in special ed. class. Will Kenny Marks still be eating peanut butter and onion sandwiches? Will Mrs. Crowell be my teacher again? Will she have forgotten about my garter snake or will she still jump whenever the steam heating cuts in?

You see, the worries are endless. But this year I decided was going to be different. This year I wasn't going to worry or fret or stew about anything. I would go into grade six with a new approach. How was I going to do that, you ask? Simple. I wasn't going to go.

I bounced this idea off Mom on the last day of summer vacation, but she bounced it right back. She stopped canning dill pickles and looked at me like I had just said I was going to give up breathing.

"Oh, Frieda," she said, "don't be so silly! Of

course you're going to school."

I shook my head stubbornly. "No, I'm not! I'm never going back." Something in my voice reminded me of the gangsters in those old movies, the ones who break out of prison and swear they're never going back to the "big house." I liked the effect.

Mom continued her canning, but I knew she wasn't going to give in easily. "Would you like to tell me why?" she asked.

"Because I'm not well," I said. "I'm a sick person."

"You're telling me," muttered Stanley. He was sitting at the table reading a comic book, but he looked up in time to catch my 'who asked you, wombat?' look.

"I'm serious," I said to Mom. "I'm sick. I think I got schistosomiasis."

Mom almost dropped a jar when she heard that one. She burst out laughing.

"What's so funny?" I demanded.

"Frieda, you don't even know what schistosomiasis is," she said between guffaws.

I glared at her indignantly. "I do so! I read about it in *Readers' Digest*. It's a really gross disease. You get these grody worm-like things in your blood and they eat you from the inside out."

"Hey, Margot, that's what you need," piped in Stanley. "You're always wanting to lose weight."

Margot left the makeup mirror she was worshipping and sneaked up behind Stanley. With one quick thrust she rammed her open tube of lipstick in his ear. "Never think again," she warned. "Your brain won't stand the pressure."

Before Stanley could threaten, "I'm gonna kill you!" Mom stepped in.

"All right, knock it off!" she ordered. She pulled a tissue out of the box on the fridge and handed it to Stanley. Then she said to me, "Frieda, schistosomiasis is a disease you get from walking in the irrigation ditches in Egypt. Have you been there lately?"

She had me on that one. "Well, no," I said, "but yesterday I stepped on a pair of Stanley's dirty jockey shorts with my bare foot. You never know what you might catch from those."

"Nice try," she said. "Have fun in grade six."

I crumpled in my chair and moaned, "Oh, Mom! Why don't you ever believe me? You never believe me!"

She smiled her superior smile. I was really getting sick of seeing it. "That's because I'm your mother," she said. "I'm used to all your crazy stories when school's starting. Last year you said you needed a heart transplant. I know you don't want to go to school."

Dad wandered into the kitchen and opened the refrigerator. "Who doesn't want to go to school?" he asked as he rummaged through the shelves for a snack.

"Frieda. Who else?" said Mom. "She's trying to get me to believe she's got some terrible disease so she can stay home tomorrow."

"I thought she had a heart condition?"

"That was last year."

Dad finally found a piece of sausage and sniffed it like a fine cigar. "Don't worry, kiddo. You're just a little nervous, that's all," he said, patting me on the head. If I was a dog I would have bitten him. "Once you get into the swing of things all your worries will seem silly. I guarantee it. Why, when I was young the first day of school was always so exciting. I remember it as the most exciting day of the year."

Then *you* go, I thought as he retreated into the living room. It was obvious I wasn't going to get any sympathy here, so I went downstairs to my room to start stewing again.

The strange thing about worrying is, the more you do, the better you get at it. By late afternoon I was in great shape. I wasn't just nervous about starting grade six, I was downright petrified. It was such a big jump. I mean, the senior grade in elementary. Awesome! There was no way I could do it. I had enough trouble getting through grade five. How was I ever going to make it in grade six? I broke out in a cold sweat.

Why couldn't I be more like Margot and Stanley? I wondered. They have no trouble in school. That's probably because they're so much smarter than me. Well, sort of. Stanley is a whiz at geometry. He can tear apart any triangle and find all the angles in three seconds flat. But ask him to make change for a dollar and he's stumped. Margot is a little better. Last year she passed food science with honours, but I think all that means is she can butter toast without having to alert the fire department first.

Oh, well, whatever the difference between us, I knew there was no way I could avoid school. I'd have to go, and that was that. Maybe Dad was right, I thought. Maybe once I got into the swing of things I'd feel better. I went to my dresser and started going through the stack of school supplies piled on top. Unfortunately as I packed my new binders with fresh paper I could only think about the hours of homework that would have to go into filling them. So I gave up on that and went to my closet. I tried to pick out something nice to wear for the first day, but in my present mood I decided any colour other than black would be tacky. After that I got into bed and waited for the end of the world.

It wasn't too long before Mom found me moping. This time she really got on my case. She said I was too old to be acting so silly about school. She told me if I didn't cheer up and put a smile on my face, she was going to give me something to be depressed about. Promises, promises, I thought, and went upstairs. With any luck I would trip and break my leg.

After supper Marcy came over and we went out for a walk. It was good to get away from Mom for a while — I was getting cramps in my lips from smiling so much. We took Cuddles with us and walked down my back alley. The evening air was cool and held the sweet/sour smell of ripening gardens and crabapples. Somewhere in the distance we heard an owl.

Before long Marcy noticed my depression and asked me what was wrong. I told her about my day and how I was worried about grade six. When I finished she rolled her eyes up in her head and started laughing. I glared at her.

"If one more person laughs at me today I'm

gonna bop them!" I warned. "This is serious."

Her smile immediately vanished, and she had the good sense to look apologetic. "Sorry, Frieda," she said. "It's just that I don't understand what your problem is. Grade six hasn't even started yet, and already you're worried about the trouble you're going to have."

"Well, don't you think I should? School isn't exactly my best subject, you know. I had a lot of problems in grade five."

"But you passed."

"That was an accident! The teachers probably did that just so they can fail me really good in grade six." I threw my hands up to the sky in desperation. "Oh, Marcy, what am I going to do? I just know I'm gonna fail. I'll probably be the only girl to graduate from elementary with white hair and false teeth!"

Marcy promptly clipped me on the head. It was a gesture she always used to get me thinking straight. "Frieda, will you just shut up and listen for a minute?" she ordered. "You're not going to fail. Read my lips. You're going to do fine."

"Yeah, yeah," I mumbled.

"Look, they passed Kenny Marks, didn't they? If the teachers think that wingnut can handle grade six they must figure you're a genius!"

I was silent for a moment. I hadn't thought about that. Kenny Marks really wasn't very bright in school. Last year in science class we were studying animal hair under the microscope, and he brought in a bagful he had shaved off his mom's mink coat. Compared to him I did seem pretty smart.

I looked at Marcy, hope returning. "You think so?" I asked.

Marcy smiled confidently. "I know so. You're gonna make it, Frieda. Remember what I told you when school let out? You're a survivor. Face it."

A survivor. The words sounded as strange now as the first time she had said them to me. But how did she know? What made her so certain I was a survivor? I wanted to ask her, but I knew she'd clip me again, so I kept quiet.

That night at my house everyone went to bed early. Dad said it was going to be a busy day for all of us tomorrow, and frankly I was pooped. It's strange how worrying can wear a person out more than work. As I got undressed and put on my pyjamas a shrill scream echoed through the house. It was Margot.

"Help! Help!" she cried. "There's a spider in my room! I think it's a black widow!"

"Not so loud," grumbled Dad. "The neighbours'll want one."

"Very funny! Are you gonna, like, lie there, or are you gonna come in here and kill it?"

"Whatcha gonna do, Dad? Huh? Squash it?" asked Stanley.

"No, I thought I'd take it out for supper and a little dancing after. What do you think?"

"Can I watch?"

"Richard," said Mom groggily, "what is it? Where are you going?"

"Crazy. Want to come along?"

I crawled into bed and listened to the footsteps tracking overhead. Suddenly a warm, comforting feeling spread over me, and I knew at last that Marcy was right. "I *am* a survivor," I said to myself. "I survived a whole summer vacation with them, didn't I?" What other proof did I need?

I turned off the light and snuggled under the blankets. Cripes, I thought, I might even be invincible.